RUTH R

Classic British crime... and Ruth Rendell is crime fiction at its very best. Ingenious and meticulous plots, subtle and penetrating characterizations, beguiling storylines and wry observations have all combined to put her at the very top of her craft.

Her first novel, *From Doon with Death*, appeared in 1964, and since then her reputation and readership has grown steadily with each new book. She has now received four major awards for her work: an Edgar from the Mystery Writers of America; Current Crime's silver cup for the best British crime novel of 1975 for *Shake Hands Forever*; the Crime Writer's Association's Gold Dagger for 1976's best crime novel for *A Demon in My View*; and the Arts Council National Book Award for Genre Fiction in 1981 for *Lake of Darkness*.

Ruth Rendell's novels have received outstanding reviews

'Ruth Rendell is really first-class . . . a natural story-teller' *Times Literary Supplement*

'The appearance of any novel by Ruth Rendell is a cause for celebration' *Spectator*

'Ruth Rendell's superb crime novels make her my favourite to inherit the title Queen of Crime' Graham Lord, *Sunday Express*

'Britain's new Queen of Crime' *Daily Mirror*

RUTH RENDELL

A GUILTY THING SURPRISED

ARROW BOOKS

Arrow Books Limited
17–21 Conway Street, London W1P 5HL

An imprint of the Hutchinson Publishing Group

London Melbourne Sydney Auckland
Johannesburg and agencies
throughout the world

First published by Hutchinson 1970

Arrow edition 1980

Reprinted 1982

© Ruth Rendell 1970

Made and printed in Great Britain
by The Anchor Press Ltd
Tiptree, Essex

ISBN 0 09 923500 5

For Michael Richards,
my cousin, with love

High instincts, before which our mortal nature
Did tremble like a guilty thing surprised;
      .... those first affections,
     Those shadowy recollections,
     Which, be they what they may,
Are yet the fountain light of all our day . . .

                William Wordsworth

1

WHEN Quentin Nightingale left home for London each morning his wife was always still asleep. His housekeeper served him with breakfast, opened the front door for him and handed him his hat and his umbrella, while the *au pair* girl fetched his newspaper. Next to speed him on his way were the two gardeners, saluting him with a respectful 'Good morning, sir', then perhaps his brother-in-law, hurrying to the sequestered peace of his writer's haven in the Old House. Only Elizabeth was missing, but if Quentin minded he never showed it. He walked briskly and confidently towards his car like a happy man.

On this particular morning in early September everything was just as usual except that Quentin didn't need his umbrella. The gardens of Myfleet Manor lay half-veiled by a golden mist which promised a beautiful day. Quentin came down the stone steps from the front door and paused briefly in the shrubbery to remind Will Palmer that the incurved chrysanthemums they were nursing for Kingsmarkham flower show were due for a dose of liquid fertiliser. Then he followed the path to the courtyard between the old coach-houses, where his car, its windscreen newly polished by Sean Lovell, stood waiting.

Quentin was a little early. Instead of getting into his car, he strolled to the low wall and looked down over the Kingsbrook valley. The view never ceased to delight him.

Hardly another house was visible, only the meadows, green, and, those that had been newly shorn, pale gold; the river winding through its thin sleeve of willows; the low round hills each topped with its ring of trees, and there, to his left, on the other side of the road, the great fir forest. It covered a whole range of hills and this morning in the mist it looked like a dark velvet cloak flung carelessly across the landscape. Quentin was always thinking of metaphors for the forest, comparing it to something, romanticising it. Sometimes he thought of it not as a forest or a velvet cloak but as a recumbent animal, guarding the fields while it slept, and of those irradiating plantations as spread, powerful and protective paws.

He turned his gaze to his own parkland, then to the nearer grounds, the sleek misted lawns and the massed roses whose colours were made pallid by haze, and he was just considering whether he should take a rose, an Iceberg perhaps or a Super Star, when a finger touched his shoulder and a cool voice said:

'To her fair works did Nature link
The human soul that through me ran;
And much it grieved my heart to think
What man has made of man.'

'Good morning, Denys,' Quentin said heartily. 'Not a very cheerful quotation to make on a lovely morning. Wordsworth, isn't it?'

Denys Villiers nodded. 'If I'm not cheerful,' he said, 'it must be because term begins in two days' time and after that I shan't get any more work done till Christmas. By the way, I've something for you.' He opened his briefcase and brought out a book, new, glossy, evidently fresh from the binders. 'An advance copy,' he said. 'I thought you might like it.'

Quentin's face lit with pleasure. He read the title: *Wordsworth in Love*, by Denys Villiers, and then, with barely controlled excitement, he turned to the dedication. This he read aloud. ' *"For my brother-in-law, Quentin Nightingale, a true friend and patron."* Ah, Denys, that's wonderful! Makes me feel like Southampton.'

Villiers gave one of his crooked, rare smiles. 'The only begetter of these ensuing essays, Mr Q.N. . . .' He frowned, as if at his own weakness. 'As long as you like it. Well, as I have work to do and so do you . . .'

'Yes, I must be off. Look after yourself, Denys. I shan't be able to wait to get home and start on this.' He tapped the book, patted Villiers' shoulder and turned away. Villiers pushed open the door in the Old House wall and entered the shady court where limes and cypresses grew and where the sun never penetrated. Still smiling, his present on the seat beside him, Quentin drove away to London.

Elizabeth Nightingale spent an hour preparing herself for the eyes of the world. The effect aimed at was one of simple youth, spotless, fresh, lightly painted, dressed with casual precision or perhaps precise casualness. People said she looked no more than twenty-five. Ah, said Elizabeth to her reflection, but they didn't know me when I was twenty-five! Sometimes she also said that nowadays it took her twice as long to look half as good.

Ever-democratic, she took her morning coffee with the staff in the kitchen. The two gardeners sat at either end of the table and Elizabeth sat opposite Katje Doorn. Mrs Cantrip drank her coffee standing up, issuing her orders. 'If you catch sight of that Alf Tawney, Will, mind you tell him I've got a chicken ordered for tonight and I want it this morning, not five minutes before Madam's dinnertime. Take your elbows off the table, young Sean. If I've told you once, I've told you fifty times. Now, Catcher, when you've drunk your coffee you can take Mr Villiers' over to him. He'll think we're all dead and that's a fact. And, for pity's sake, turn off that radio. Madam doesn't want to listen to that racket, I'm sure.'

'Oh, but I like pop, Mrs Cantrip,' said Elizabeth.

Sean lifted his head. 'Only got to look at you,' he said, 'to see you're no square.'

Shocked, Mrs Cantrip said, 'That's no way to talk to Madam!'

'I take it as a great compliment,' said Elizabeth.

Sean's dark face flushed with pleasure and he smiled his pomegranate smile, showing even white teeth between red lips. Inspired by his employer's encouragement, he eyed first Mrs Cantrip and then Will Palmer. Katje was giggling, but he ignored her. 'You're all the same, you oldies,' he said, 'stuck in the same old groove.'

'Your groove's gardening and don't you forget it. You'll never be one of them singers.'

'And why not?' But Sean's aggressive mood had changed to despair. 'I'll have to get cracking, I'll just have to. I said to my old lady, Time's getting on, I'll be twenty-three come April. What would have happened if the Beatles had waited till they was twenty-three before making a start?'

'What would have happened?' said Mrs Cantrip. 'The world'd have been a quieter place and that's a fact.'

'Never mind, Sean,' said Elizabeth with her sweet smile. 'You know what I've promised. I won't forget.' And Sean nodded eagerly, watching Elizabeth with rapt eyes. 'Now, Will, there's a suit Mr Nightingale's finished with that

12

might fit you. While I'm in the giving vein, I've packed up a little parcel for your mother, Katje. Some of those biscuits she can't get in Holland. You'll find it on the hall table with a parcel of mine. Perhaps you'd take them to the post?'

'Madam,' said Mrs Cantrip when Elizabeth had gone, 'is an angel. It's a crying shame there aren't more like her about.'

Katje giggled.

The mist had lifted and the rooms of Myfleet Manor were full of light—strong, late summer sunlight that would show up the slightest vestige of dust. But Mrs Cantrip and Katje had been at work and there was no dust. Elizabeth walked from room to room across the thick smooth sun-bathed carpets, checking that the flowers in copper bowls and *famille rose* vases were still fresh, occasionally drawing a curtain to protect old delicate satin from the sun. From her bedroom window she watched Katje cross Myfleet village street, holding the two parcels, the one for Holland and the one for London in her plump pink hands. Elizabeth sighed. Almost any of her friends or her servants would have supposed she sighed because Katje had left both the gates—wrought-iron gates whose design was of wyverns rampant with snouts which should have met at the lock—wide open. On the bright white surface of the road Katje's shadow was black and bouncy, a little deformed by the bulges the parcels made.

Elizabeth went down and closed the gates. She got into the Lotus, driving first to Queens Waterford to discuss with Lady Larkin-Smith the arrangements for the country club dance, next to Pomfret to receive from Mrs Rogers the proceeds from the Cancer Relief collection, lastly to the hairdresser's in Kingsmarkham. She kept the windows of the car wide open, the top down, and her primrose pale hair streamed out behind her as she drove, like the thistle-down hair of a young girl.

At half past one Mrs Cantrip served luncheon in the dining room. Katje's status gave her the right to eat *en famille*, but in the absence of Quentin Nightingale she said little. The woman and the girl ate their asparagus, their ham and their blackberry shortcake, in a silence which Elizabeth occasionally broke to comment with pleasure on the food. When they had finished Katje said she would have preferred chipolata pudding.

'You must teach Mrs Cantrip to make it.'

'Perhaps I am teaching her this afternoon,' said Katje, who had difficulties with her present tense.

'What a good idea!'

'When you are tasting it perhaps you never wish black-berries again.' Katje poked about in her mouth, retrieving seeds from between her teeth.

'We shall have to see. I'm going up for my rest now. If anyone calls or telephones, remember, I'm not to be disturbed.'

'I am remembering,' said Katje.

'Were you thinking of going out tonight?'

'I meet a boy in Kingsmarkham and maybe we go to the movies.'

'Cinema or pictures, Katje,' said Elizabeth gently. 'You must only say movies when you're in the United States. You can take one of the cars if you like but I'd rather you didn't take the Lotus. Your mother wouldn't like to think of you driving a fast sports car.'

'I am taking the Mini, please?'

'That's right.'

Katje cleared the table and put the crockery in the dish-

14

washer with the glass and the plates from Denys Villiers' luncheon tray. 'Now I am teaching you to make chipolata pudding,' she announced to Mrs Cantrip, who had been taking ten minutes off with a cup of tea and the *Daily Sketch.*

'And what might that be when it's at home? You know Madam never has no sausages in this house.'

'Is not sausages. Is cream and jelly and fruit. We have cream, yes? We have eggs? Come on now, Mrs Cantrip, dear.'

'There's no peace for the wicked and that's a fact,' said Mrs Cantrip, heaving herself out of her rocking chair. 'Though what's wrong with a good English dessert I never shall know. Mr Villiers ate up every scrap of his. Mind you, with all that book-writing he gets a hearty appetite.'

Katje fetched eggs and cream from the refrigerator. 'Often I am asking myself,' she said thoughtfully, 'why he is not working in his own home. When he has a wife too, is odd, very funny.'

'And might I ask what it's got to do with you, Catcher? The fact is Mr Villiers has always worked up there. It must be fourteen or fifteen years since Mr Nightingale had the Old House done up for Mr Villiers to work in. It's quiet, see? And Mr Nightingale's got a very soft spot for Mr Villiers.'

'A soft spot?'

'I don't know, these foreigners! I mean he likes him, he's fond of him. I reckon he's proud of having an author in the family. Switch the beater on, then.'

Tipping the cream into a bowl, Katje said, 'Mrs Nightingale is not liking him *at all.* Every day in the holidays he is working up there and never, not once, Mrs Nightingale is going to see him. Is funny not to like her own brother.'

'Maybe he's not easy to like,' said Mrs Cantrip. 'You can depend on it, if there's a quarrel—and I'm not saying there is, mind—it's not Madam's fault. He's got a very funny manner with him, has Mr Villiers. A nasty temper, like sarcastic. Between you and me, Catcher, I wouldn't be too happy if I had a boy at that school where he teaches. Now switch that thing off or the cream'll all be turned to butter.'

Elizabeth didn't appear for tea.

The sky was cloudless, like a Mediterranean sky, and the sun, at five, as hot as ever. Out in the grounds Will Palmer lit a bonfire down by the gate which led on to the Kingsmarkham road, fouling the warm, scented air with acrid smoke. He fed it with grass mowings and helped it occasionally with a drop of paraffin. Sweating and grumbling, Sean pushed the motor mower over the terraced lawns.

Mrs Cantrip laid the dining table and left a cold dinner on the trolley. Fair weather or foul, she always wore a hat when she went outside. She put it on now and went home to her cottage at the other end of the village.

In the Old House Denys Villiers typed three more sentences on Wordsworth and the emergence of nature as artistic inspiration, and then he too went home. He drove slowly and cautiously to his bungalow in Clusterwell, to be followed half an hour later by Katje Doorn, revving up the Mini and making it roar and squeal its way through the villages to Kingsmarkham.

Elizabeth lay on her bed with witch-hazel pads on her eyes, conserving her beauty. When she heard the Jaguar come in she began to dress for dinner.

She wore a pale green caftan with crystal embroidery at the neck and wrists.

'How's my beautiful wife?'

'I'm fine, darling. Had a good day?'

'Not so bad. London's like a hothouse. Can I get you a drink?'

'Just a small tomato juice,' said Elizabeth. Quentin poured it for her and for himself a double whisky. 'Thank you, darling. It *is* hot, isn't it?'

'Not so hot as in London.'

'No, I suppose not.'

'Not nearly so hot,' said Quentin firmly. He smiled; she smiled. Silence fell.

Quentin broke it. 'Katje not about?'

'She's taken the Mini into Kingsmarkham, darling.'

'All on our own then, are we? No one coming in for cocktails?'

'Not tonight. As you say, we're all on our own.'

Quentin sighed and smiled. 'Makes a pleasant change, really,' he said, 'to be on our own.'

Elizabeth made no reply. This time the silence was intense and of longer duration. Quentin stood by the window and looked at the garden.

'We may as well have dinner,' said Elizabeth at last.

In the dining room he opened a bottle of *Pouilly Fuissé*. Elizabeth took only one glass.

'Turning cooler at last,' said Quentin during the *vichy-soisse*. 'I suppose the nights will soon be drawing in.'

'I suppose they will.'

'Yes, no matter how hot it is at this time of the year, you always feel that faint nip in the air.' Elizabeth ate her cold chicken in silence. 'But it's been a good summer on the whole,' Quentin said desperately.

'On the whole.'

Presently they returned to the drawing room.

'What time is it?' asked Quentin from the french windows.

'Just on eight.'

'Really? I should have said it was much later.' He went out on to the terrace to look at his chrysanthemums. Elizabeth looked at *Queen* magazine, turning the pages indifferently. Quentin came back and sat looking at her. Then he said, 'I wonder if Denys and Georgina will look in?'

'I shouldn't think so.'

'I think I'll give Denys a ring and see if they'll come over for a hand of bridge. What do you think?'

'If you'd like it, darling.'

'No, no, it's up to you.'

'I really don't mind one way or the other, darling.'

'Well, I'll just give him a ring, then,' said Quentin, expelling pent-up breath in a long sigh.

The Villiers arrived and they played bridge till ten.

'We mustn't be too late, Georgina,' said Villiers, looking at his watch. 'I've got a couple of hours' work to put in at the school library before I go to bed.'

'What, again?' said Georgina.

'I told you earlier, I've got a reference to look up.'

His wife gave him a mutinous glare.

'Denys is dedicated to his work,' said Quentin, the peacemaker. He smiled kindly at Georgina as the women left the room. 'Talking of dedications,' he said to his brother-in-law, 'will you write in the book for me?'

Using a broken old ballpoint, Denys Villiers wrote on the flyleaf:

The thought of our past years in me doth breed
Perpetual benediction . . .

Quentin read it and a faint flush of pleasure coloured his cheeks. He laid his hand on Villiers' shoulder. 'Now write your name,' he said.

So Villiers wrote beneath the quotation: *Your brother, Denys Villiers.*

'It's not like you to be inaccurate. It ought to be "brother-in-law".'

'There's no need,' said Villiers sharply, shaking off the hand, 'for too much bloody accuracy.'

The women came back, Georgina fastening her large handbag.

'Thanks very much for letting me have this, Elizabeth,' said Georgina. 'It's awfully good of you.'

'You're more than welcome, my dear. I shall never use it again.' And Elizabeth kissed her affectionately.

'When you've finished billing and cooing,' said Denys Villiers unpleasantly, 'perhaps we can get a move on.'

'I think I'll go straight to bed,' said Quentin. 'I can't wait to start the new book. Are you going to sit up a bit longer?'

'It's such a fine evening,' said Elizabeth. 'I may have a walk in the grounds before I go to bed.'

'Wrap up warm, darling. I'll say good night, then.'

'Good night, darling.'

Elizabeth fetched herself a coat, a soft lightweight thing of deep green angora. In the moonlight it was the same colour as the cypresses that grew in the Italian garden. Late blooming roses, pink, apricot, lemon, all looked white tonight. She walked across the turf between the rosebeds, hexagonal, semicircular, rhomboid, then by the paved path between yew hedges to a door in the red brick wall. The smoke from Will's fire rose in a thin grey column.

Elizabeth unlocked the gate and let herself out on to the grass verge which, overhung by the Manor beeches, separated the wall from the Pomfret road. As car headlights flared, flowed past, she stepped back for a moment into the shadows of the garden. Katje in the Mini, coming home from Kingsmarkham. Once more the road was empty, lighted only by the moon. Elizabeth closed the gate behind her, crossed the road and began to walk away from it by a sandy path that led into Cheriton Forest.

When she was out of sight of the road she sat down on a log, waiting. Presently she lit a cigarette, the third of the five she would smoke that day.

The Nightingales slept in separate bedrooms on the first floor of Myfleet Manor and at the front of the house. Quentin undressed and got into bed quickly. He switched on his bedlamp and opened *Wordsworth in Love*.

First, as was his custom with Villiers' books, he studied with pride and pleasure the publisher's eulogy of the author and his works, and scrutinised his brother-in-law's portrait on the back of the jacket. Next he looked at all the illustrations in turn, the photographed paintings of Wordsworth, of his sister Dorothy, and of the 'mazy Forth' as seen from Stirling Castle. Then, finally, he began to read.

Quentin read like a scholar, religiously looking up every bibliographical reference and reading each footnote. He had just come to the poet's meeting with his French sweetheart when he heard footsteps on the stairs. Elizabeth in from her walk? But no . . .

The footsteps went on, up and up, until they sounded faintly above his head. Not Elizabeth, then, but Katje who slept on the top floor.

It was eleven-thirty and growing chilly. He had said

earlier that there was a nip in the air. Elizabeth would be cold out there in the garden. The sashes in his own windows and the casements up above rattled as the wind rose. Quentin laid aside his book, got up and looked out of the window.

The moon had disappeared behind a bank of cloud. He put on his dressing gown, opened the bedroom door and stood for a moment in perplexity before making for the stairs.

2

I^T was Detective Inspector Michael Burden's day off. He lay in bed till nine. Then he got up, bathed, and began on the task to which he intended to devote this free day, painting the outside of his bungalow.

A great wind, offshoot of a Caribbean hurricane the Americans called Caroline, had arisen during the night. Burden needed to use no ladders; the eaves of his bungalow were too near the ground for that, but today he didn't even fancy ascending the steps. Certainly he wasn't going to allow his eleven-year-old son John, home for the school holidays and an enthusiastic helper, to go up them.

'You can do the front door, John,' he said, knowing that he was conferring a special favour. All painters, particularly amateurs, long for the moment when the top coat, an excitingly contrasting colour, is due to be applied to the front door.

'Blimey, can I?' said John.

'Don't say blimey. It means God blind me, and you know I don't like to hear you swear.'

John, who normally would have argued the point, trotted off to fetch from the garage a virgin pot of flamingo-pink paint. There he encountered his sister Pat, feeding lime leaves to a hawk-moth caterpillar imprisoned in a shoe box. He was about to say something calculated to aggravate, something on the lines of the folly of encouraging garden pests, when his mother called to him from the back door.

'John, tell Daddy he's wanted on the phone, will you?'

'Who wants him?'

Mrs Burden said in a voice of resigned despair, 'Can't you guess?'

John guessed. Carrying the tin of paint, he returned to his father, who had just put the first stroke of top coat on the picture-window frame.

'Cop shop on the phone for you,' he said.

Burden never swore, in front of his children or in their absence. Carefully he placed his brush in a jam jar of synthetic turps and entered the house.

His bungalow had seldom looked so attractive to him as it did this morning. Poole pottery vases filled with red dahlias (Bishop of Llandaff, very choice) graced the hall and living room; the new curtains were up; from the kitchen came the rich aroma of a steak-and-kidney pudding boiling for lunch. Burden sighed, then lifted the spotless polished receiver of the white telephone.

The voice of Detective Chief Inspector Wexford said nastily, 'You took your bloody time.'

'Sorry. I was painting.'

'Hard cheese, Picasso. You'll have to complete the masterpiece some other time. Duty calls.'

Burden knew better than to say it was his day off. 'What's up, sir?'

'Do you know a Mrs Elizabeth Nightingale?'

'By sight. Everyone knows her. Husband's a Lloyd's underwriter. Pots of money. What's she done?'

'Got herself murdered, that's what she's done.'

Burden broke his rule. 'Good God!' he said.

'I'm at Myfleet Manor. Get over here as soon as you can, Mike.'

'And I've made this great enormous pudding,' said Jean Burden. 'Try and get back for lunch.'

'Not a hope.' Burden changed his clothes, grabbed his car key. John was sitting on the garden wall, waiting for starter's orders. 'Better leave the front door for a day or two, John. Sorry about that.'

'I'd be O.K. on my own.'

'Don't argue, there's a good lad.' He fished in his pocket for a half-crown. 'You were saying something about a new transistor battery . . . Get yourself some sweets too.' He got into the car. 'Here, John—isn't a Mr Villiers that's brother to Mrs Nightingale a teacher at your school?'

'Old Roman Villa?' said John. 'I don't know whose brother he is. He teaches Latin and Greek. What d'you want to know for?'

'Oh, nothing,' said Burden.

It was a red-brick house, built during the reign of Queen Anne, and it had an air of crouching close above the road, its windows Argus eyes that gazed down over the village, its footings embowered in thick green shrubs which rustled in the wind. Burden parked his car behind the bigger official one Wexford had arrived in, pushed open the wyvern gates and mounted the steps to the front door. Detective Sergeant Martin opened it before he had a chance to ring the bell.

'Chief Inspector's in the—er, what they call the morning room, sir.'

The house was full of people and yet a thick breathless hush seemed to hang over it, the silence of the incredible, the silence of shock. Burden tapped on the morning-room door and went in.

It was a small elegant room, its panelling painted in cream and blue. A broad shelf followed the line of the picture rail on which stood floral plates in blue Delft. There were water-colours too, delicate pictures of pastoral scenes—Myfleet Mill, Forby Church, the river bridge at Flagford.

Squeezed into a small chair upholstered in cream satin, Wexford looked even more mountainous than usual. His heavy face was grave but his eyes were alert and watchful, fixed on the woman who sat on the opposite side of the fireplace. Glancing at the neat white hair, the homely red face furrowed by tears and the trim blue nylon overall, Burden summed her up as a faithful servant, an old and devoted retainer.

'Come in,' said Wexford. 'Sit down. This is Mrs Cantrip. She has kept house for Mr and Mrs Nightingale since they were married sixteen years ago.'

'That's right, sir,' said Mrs Cantrip, putting a handkerchief up to her swollen eyes. 'And a lovelier person than Mrs Nightingale you couldn't wish to meet. Good as gold she was and the best I ever worked for. I often used to think, though it don't sound respectful, pity it's me and not her who might be wanting a reference one of these days. I could have painted it in glowing colours and that's a fact.'

Burden sat down gingerly on another satin chair. All the furnishings were spotless and exquisite from the gleaming china to the lady's firescreens, painted oval discs on long stems.

'I'm sure I don't know what you must think of us, sir,' said Mrs Cantrip, misinterpreting his expression. 'The place in the state it is, but nothing's been done this morning. Me and Catcher, we haven't felt up to lifting a duster. When they told me the news I felt so bad I don't know why I didn't pass clean out.' She turned to Wexford and sniffed back her tears. 'Well, sir, you said as you wanted to see everyone in the house, so I mustn't keep you now the other gentleman's come.' Counting on work-worn fingers, she said, 'There's old Will Palmer, him that found her poor dead body, and Sean Lovell and Catcher . . .'

'Who's Catcher?'

'The foreign girl, what they call an *au pair*, sir. You'll find her up in her room on the top floor. And then there's poor Mr Nightingale himself, locked in his study and won't open the door to no one.'

'I will see Mr Palmer first,' said Wexford.

'How long have you been here?' asked Burden. The sepulchral silence of the place made him feel that whispering was in order.

'Since seven-thirty,' said Wexford, keeping his own voice low as they followed Mrs Cantrip down a long passage and into the garden via the kitchen. 'Thank you, Mrs Cantrip. I think I can see Mr Palmer coming up to meet us.'

The grounds were being searched by men in uniform and men in plain clothes. Will Palmer, emerging from behind a macrocarpa hedge, stopped in the middle of the lawn, looking surly, as Constable Gates grubbed among the flower-pots in one of the greenhouses, and Constable Bryant, his shirt-sleeves rolled up, thrust his arms into the green depths of the lily pond.

'The body has been photographed and removed,' said Wexford. 'Someone hit her on the head. God knows what with. They're looking for the weapon now. There was a hell of a lot of blood.' He raised his voice. 'Mr Palmer! Will you come over here, please?'

He was a tall lean old man with hard fleshless features that the wind and weather had polished to the tint of rosewood. Dark red, too, was the bald spot on his crown, a daisy centre amid white petals.

'I reckoned you'd want a word with me,' he said with lugubrious importance. 'What's all this poking about in my garden in aid of?'

'We are searching,' said Wexford frankly, 'for the weapon that killed Mrs Nightingale.'

'Don't reckon you'll find it among my fuchsias.'

'That remains to be seen.' Wexford pointed in the direction of a thin column of smoke. 'How long has that bonfire been burning?'

'Since yesterday afternoon, governor.'

'I see. Where can we go and talk, Mr Palmer? How about the kitchen, or will Mrs Cantrip be there?'

'Like enough she will, governor, and she's got mighty long ears when she wants. We could go in the Italian garden, being as it's sheltered from the wind.'

They sat down on a long seat of metal scrollwork beside a formal pool whose waters were still muddy from the investigations of its bottom by Wexford's men. At the far end of this pool was an elaborate baroque structure with a niche in which stood a bronze boy pouring water from a flagon into a bowl. The whole garden measured perhaps thirty feet by twenty and it was surrounded by cypress trees which shivered in the wind.

'Well, it was like this,' said Palmer. 'That old wind come up in the night, making such a racket it was, it woke me up. Near enough about four-thirty. First thing I thought of was Mr Nightingale's chrysanths, them as we're getting ready for the flower show. They was standing out in the open in their pots, see, and I thought, That wind'll have them over, sure as Fate. So I got on my bike and I come up here, quick as I could.'

'What time did you get here, Mr Palmer?'

' 'Bout five.' Palmer spoke slowly and with relish. It was evident he was beginning to enjoy himself. 'Them chrysanths was all standing up well to the wind but I put them in the greenhouse to be on the safe side. Then I saw something was up. I couldn't believe my eyes. One of them french windows was wide open. Burglars, I thought. They've had burglars. I didn't rightly know what to do for the best. Maybe it's just that old wind, I thought, and they've forgot to lock up. Still, I reckoned it was my duty to wake Mr Nightingale, so in I went and up the stairs and banged and banged on his bedroom door. Must be a real heavy sleeper, I thought to myself, and I took the liberty of going in to have a look.'

'He was there?'

'No, he weren't. His bed was empty. "Mr Nightingale," I said, "are you there, sir?" thinking he might be in his bathroom, the door being shut . . .'

'But you didn't look?' Wexford interrupted as he paused for breath.

'I hope I know my place, sir. Besides . . .' Palmer looked down at his darned and shiny trouser knees. 'Besides, for all they slept separate like, they was married and . . .'

'You thought quite reasonably that he might have spent the night in Mrs Nightingale's room?'

'Well, governor, I did at that. I always have said the gentry have their funny ways as the likes of us don't understand.' Giving no sign of embarrassment at his perhaps inadvertent inclusion of Wexford and Burden among the hoi-polloi, Palmer went on, 'So, not getting no answer from Mr Nightingale, I took it upon myself to knock on Madam's door. Nobody come and I was beginning to get the wind up, I can tell you. A proper state I was in. Nothing else would have got me barging into a lady's bedroom, and me just a servant like and in me working things. Well, she wasn't there either and the bed not touched.'

'You didn't think of calling the *au pair* girl?'

'Never crossed my mind, governor. What could that Catcher do I couldn't do myself? I went round the grounds then and found the wall gate open. Best get on the phone to the police yourself, Will, I thought, but when I got back to the house Mr Nightingale was up and about. Been having a bath, he said, and when he'd dried himself and come out I was gone.'

'What happened next?' asked Burden.

Palmer scratched his head. 'Mr Nightingale said Madam must have met with an accident while she was out in the grounds, but I said I'd searched the grounds. Then,' he said, building up suspense like an experienced narrator, 'I thought of that open gate and that dark old forest and my heart turned over. "I reckon she went into the forest and come over bad," I said to poor Mr Nightingale, so we went into the forest, our hearts in our mouths like, and I went first and then I found her. Lying face down she was with blood all over her lovely golden hair. But you saw her, governor. You know.'

'Thank you, Mr Palmer. You've been very helpful.'

'I always try to do my duty, sir. Mr Nightingale's been real good to me and Madam too. There's some I could name as would take advantage, but not me. I reckon I belong to what they call the old school.'

Wexford glanced up and saw through the cypresses a figure leaning on a spade. 'Did Sean What's-his-name take advantage?' he asked softly.

'Lovell, governor, Sean Lovell. Well now, he did, in a manner of speaking. Folks don't know their place like what they did when I was young, and that Lovell—common as dirt he is. His mother's no better than she should be and I don't reckon he never had no father. Turn you up, it would, to see the inside of their cottage. But he fancied himself Madam's equal, if you've ever heard the like. Elizabeth this and Elizabeth that, he says to me behind her back. Don't you let me hear you refer to Madam like that, I said, snubbing him proper.'

Burden said impatiently, 'How did he take advantage?'

'Fancies himself singing in one of them pop groups, he does. Madam was soft, you see, and she'd smile and listen ever so patient when he'd start his singing. Sang to her, he did . . .' Palmer mouthed disgustedly, showing foul broken teeth. 'When she'd got a window open he'd come up underneath and sing one of them rubbishy songs he'd got off the telly. Familiar, you wouldn't believe! I come on him one day standing with Madam down by the pond here, nattering to her nineteen to the dozen and his dirty paw on her arm. I could tell Madam didn't like it. She jumped proper and went all red when I shouted at him. "A diabolical liberty," I said to him when we was alone. "Elizabeth and me, we understand each other," he says. The nerve of it!' Palmer's old bones cracked as he got to his feet and scowled in Lovell's direction. 'All I can say is,' he said, 'I hope I'm gone before all this equality gets any worse than what it is.'

Skilful conversion and the use of room dividers had transformed the largest attic into an open-plan flat for the *au pair* girl. Sleek shelves of polished beech on which stood books and house plants divided the sitting room from the sleeping area. All the furniture was modern. Vermilion tweed covered the sofa and the two armchairs; the carpet was a sour smart green; the curtains red corded velvet.

'Speak good English, do you, Miss Doorn?' Wexford asked as she admitted them.

'Oh, no, I am very bad,' said the Dutch girl, giggling.

Everybody tell me I am very very bad.' She smiled without shame.

She belonged, Wexford thought admiringly, to the classic Dutch type which, photographed in clogs and peasant dress among windmills and tulips, advertises the attractions of Holland on holiday posters. Her hair was pale gold and long, her eyes a bright frank blue and her skin as dazzling as any ivory tulip in the Keukenhof Gardens. When she laughed, and she seemed to be always laughing, her face lit up and glowed. She looked, Wexford thought, about twenty.

'How long,' he asked, 'have you been living here with Mr and Mrs Nightingale?'

'One year. Nearly one year and a half.'

'So you knew them well? You lived as one of the family?'

'There is no family,' said Katje, pushing out full pink lips in disgust. 'Just him and her.' She shrugged. 'And now he is dead.'

'Yes indeed. That is why I am here. No doubt, you were a good friend to Mrs Nightingale, like a grown-up daughter?'

Katje laughed. She curled her legs under her, bounced up and down. Then she covered her mouth, suppressing giggles, with one hand. 'Oh, I must not laugh when all is so sad! But it is so funny what you say. A daughter! Mrs Nightingale wouldn't like to hear that, I think. No, she think she is young girl, very young and pretty in little mini skirts and eye-liner on, so!'

Burden fixed her with a disapproving glare which she met with frank wide eyes. Persisting doggedly, Wexford said, 'Nevertheless, you were in her confidence?'

'Please?'

Burden came to his assistance. 'She talked to you about her life?' he said.

'Me? No, never, nothing. At lunch we sit so, she there, I here. How is your mother, Katje? Will it rain today? Now I lie down and have my little rest. But talk? No, we do not *talk*.'

'You must have been lonely.'

'Me?' The giggles broke out in fresh gusts. 'Perhaps I should be lonely . . .' She hesitated, struggling with her conditionals. 'Perhaps if I stay in all day with him and her and all evening too, then I am lonely. No, I have my friends in Kingsmarkham, many many friends, boys and girls. Why do I like to stay here with old people?'

'They were only in their forties,' said thirty-six-year-old Burden hotly.

'This,' said Katje calmly, 'is what I am saying to you. I am young, they old. Mr Nightingale, he make me laugh. He is a nice man and he say things to make me laugh, but he is old, old, older than my father in Gouda.'

Smug and secure in the unarguable possession of radiant youth, Katje smiled at Wexford, then let her eyes travel to Burden, where they lingered. She looked at him as if she were wondering whether he were obtainable. She giggled.

Blushing, Burden said sharply, 'What did you see when you came home last night?'

'Well, I am going to the movies with my friend who is a waiter at the Olive and Dove. First we see the movie, is Swedish film, very sexy, make me feel so hot, you understand?'

'Oh, yes,' said Burden, looking down.

'This is natural,' said Katje severely, 'when one is young.' She stretched her long stockingless legs and wriggled her toes in the white sandals. 'Afterwards I wish to go with my friend to his room but he will not because there is a manager at the hotel, a very unkind man, who is not letting him have girls. So we are sad and my friend takes me instead to the Carousel café. There we have coffee and one, two cakes.'

'What time was this?'

'It is a quarter to ten when we leave the movies. We are having our coffee and then we are sitting in the car, kissing and cuddling, but very sad because we cannot go to his room. My friend must rise very early in the morning, so he go back to the hotel and I go home. Now it is eleven, I think.'

'You saw Mrs Nightingale leave the Manor grounds?'

Katje poked a lock of hair into the corner of her mouth. 'Her I am seeing in the lights of the car, coming out of the gate near where the bonfire is burning. And she is seeing me too. This I know because she is closing the gate quick and hiding till I go by. Very funny, I think to myself. So I drive up along the road and I am leaving the car parked and walking back very soft, very secret, to see if she is coming out again.' Suddenly Katje sat up straight, shooting her legs out and displaying the tops of her thighs to the nervous Burden. 'She is coming out again!' she said triumphantly. 'I see her cross the road and go into the wood. And she is walking very quiet, looking like this over her shoulder.' Katje pantomimed it in a swift, curiously animal-like burlesque. 'Then I know what she is doing. Many many times have I too walked like this when I am going to meet my friend in the woods and the unkind man is not allowing us to go to his room. Over my shoulder I am looking to see that no one is following to spy what we do.'

'Yes, yes,' said Wexford gruffly. 'I understand all that.' He didn't dare look at Burden. It wouldn't altogether have surprised him if the inspector, like the man in *Bleak House*, had entirely disappeared, melting away by a process of spontaneous combustion. With more than an edge of irony to his voice, he said, 'You have been very frank with us, Miss Doorn.'

'I am good, yes?' said Katje with intense satisfaction. She chewed her hair enthusiastically. 'I tell you things that help? I am knowing all about talking with the police. When I am in Amsterdam with the provos the police are asking me many questions, so I am knowing all about police and not frightened *at all*.' She gave them a radiant smile which lingered and sparkled when it was turned on Burden. 'Now I think I am making you coffee and telling you how we throw the smoke bombs in Amsterdam while this old police chief is talking with poor Mr Nightingale.'

Burden had lost all his poise and while he stammered out something about having already had coffee, Wexford said smoothly, 'Some other time, thank you.' He didn't mind being called a police chief, but the adjective rankled. 'We shall want to talk to you again, Miss Doorn.'

'Yes, I think so too,' said Katje, giggling. Placidly she accepted the fact that most men, having once met her, would want to talk to her again. She curled up in her chair and watched them go, her eyes dancing.

'Now for Nightingale,' said Wexford as they descended the stairs. 'I've already had a few words with him but that was before I knew about these dawn ablutions of his. He'll have to come out of that study, Mike. I've sent Martin to swear a warrant to search this house.'

3

HE had the kind of looks women call distinguished. His hair was silver without a black strand and he wore a small silver moustache which gave him the look of an ambassador or a military man of high rank. Because of this rather premature silvering he looked no younger than his fifty years, although his tall figure was as slim as Sean Lovell's, his chin muscles firm and his skin unlined.

People expect a pretty woman to have a handsome husband or a rich one. Otherwise they feel the marriage is unaccountable, that she has thrown herself away. Elizabeth Nightingale had been more than usually pretty and her widower was more than usually rich besides being handsome enough to match her beauty. But this morning he looked almost ugly, his features haggard and drawn.

It had taken a good deal of persuasion and finally peremptory insistence to make him admit them to the study, but now he was inside, Wexford's anger dissolved into an impatient pity. Quentin Nightingale had been crying.

'I'm sorry, sir. I must question you just as I must question everyone else.'

'I realise that.' The voice was low, cultured and ragged. 'It was childish of me to lock myself in here. What do you want to ask me?'

35

'May we sit down?'

'Oh, please . . . I'm sorry. I should have . . .'

'I quite understand, Mr Nightingale.' Wexford sat down in a leather chair that resembled his own at the police station, and Burden chose the high wooden stool that stood by the bookcase. 'First of all, tell me about last evening. Did you and Mrs Nightingale spend it alone?'

'No. My brother-in-law and his wife came up to play bridge with us.' A little animation came into his voice as he said, 'He is the distinguished author of works on Wordsworth, you know.'

'Really?' said Wexford politely.

'They came at about eight-thirty and left at half past ten. My brother-in-law said he had some research to do at the school library before he went to bed.'

'I see. How did your wife seem last night?'

'My wife . . .' Quentin winced at the word and at having to repeat it himself. 'My wife was quite normal, gay and lovely as always.' His voice broke and he steadied it. 'A very gracious hostess. I remember she was particularly sweet to my sister-in-law. She gave her some present and Georgina was delighted. Elizabeth was the most generous of women.'

'What was this present, sir?'

'I don't know,' Quentin said, suddenly weary once more. 'I only heard Georgina thank her for it.'

Burden shifted on his stool. 'Why did your wife go into the forest, Mr Nightingale?'

'I don't know that either. My God, I wish I did. She often went for a walk in the grounds. In the late evening, I mean. I never dreamt she would go into the forest.'

'You were a happily married couple, sir?'

'Certainly we were. Ideally happy. Ask any of our

36

friends. Oh God, would I be like this, the way I am, if we hadn't been happy?'

'Please don't distress yourself, Mr Nightingale,' Wexford said gently. 'Now I want you to answer very carefully. You're aware that Palmer came into your bedroom just after five this morning but couldn't find you? Would you mind telling me where you were?'

A dark ashamed flush coloured Quentin's face. He put his hands up to his cheeks as if he thought their cold touch would drive the blood away. 'I was in the bath,' he said stiffly.

'A curious time to take a bath.'

'Occasionally we all do curious things, Chief Inspector. I awoke early on account of the wind. I couldn't get to sleep again, so I had a bath.'

'Very well, Mr Nightingale. I should like to search this house now, if you please.'

'As you like,' said Quentin. He looked like a condemned man who has received a reprieve but knows it is only a temporary stay of execution. Fingering a paperweight of dark blue stone threaded with silver, he said, 'You'll be careful, won't you?'

'We aren't vandals,' said Wexford sharply, then relenting slightly, 'Afterwards you won't know we've passed this way.'

As country houses go, Myfleet Manor wasn't large, but it wasn't, to use Burden's own phrase, a council maisonette either. Altogether there were fifteen rooms, each furnished with taste and apparently with love, nearly every one a museum of *objets d'art*. Nothing was out of place, no carpet stained or cushion crumpled. Clearly no child and certainly no dog had ever been permitted to run wild here. Only the petals fallen from flower arrangements told of half a day's neglect.

And yet, despite the dahlia-filled vases and the pale sun-beams that the wind blew flickeringly across satin and polished wood, the place had a cold sepulchral air. It was, as Wexford remarked, ascending the staircase, rather like being in church.

The life of the Manor, its pulse and the sole source of its laughter, was up above them in the *au pair* girl's flat. Glancing up the topmost flight rather wistfully, Wexford entered Quentin's bedroom, Burden following close behind.

The bed had been made. Beside it on a low table lay a book which Wexford glanced at, making no comment. He opened drawers and scanned the well-stocked ward-robe while Burden went into the bathroom.

'The bath towel's still wet, sir,' he called. 'It's on a hot rail, though, and . . .' Wexford tramped across to the bathroom where he found Burden looking at his watch. 'It wouldn't take seven hours to dry, would it?'

Wexford shook his head. 'He's either had two baths,' he said, 'or just one and that at nine or ten this morning.'

'You mean the first one was a real cleaning-up opera-tion? In that case there ought to be blood on the towel or somewhere, and there isn't.'

'We'll check the laundry with Mrs Cantrip. Let's go next door.'

The dead woman's bedroom was papered in lilac and silver, a pattern of rosebuds and blown roses which was repeated identically in the satin of the curtains. Between the two windows stood a triple-mirrored dressing table, its legs skirted in white tulle. The bed was white too, huge and smooth, flanked on either side by white fur rugs like patches of snow on the emerald field of carpet.

While Burden searched the dressing table and lifted the

lid of a writing desk, Wexford examined the wardrobe. Mrs Nightingale had possessed enough clothes to stock a boutique, the only difference between this rack and a boutique's being that these garments were all of one size, a young girl's size twelve, and they had all belonged to one woman.

'No diary,' said Burden, busy at the desk. 'A couple of receipted dressmaker's bills from a shop in Bruton Street, London, a place called Tanya Tye. The bills she's paid were for a hundred and fifty-odd and two hundred pounds, and there's a third one outstanding for another ninety-five. No interest there, I think.'

Wexford moved on to the dressing table. He lifted from its surface jars of cream, bottles of lotion, lastly a flagon of liquid whose declared purpose was to lift and brace facial muscles. 'Made out of a cow's digestive juices,' he said expressionlessly. 'Or so they tell me.' His face softened and grew sad. ' "Why such high cost," ' he quoted, ' "having so short a lease, dost thou upon thy fading mansion spend?" '

'Pardon?'

'Just a sonnet that came into my head.'

'Oh, yes?' said Burden. 'Personally, I was thinking what a waste of money when you've got to get old anyway. I don't suppose she went to all this trouble for her husband, do you?'

'No, there was another man.'

Burden nodded. 'The man she went to meet last night, presumably,' he said. 'What's your theory, sir? That Nightingale suspected, followed her into the forest and killed her? Burnt his clothes on Palmer's fire?'

'I haven't got a theory,' said Wexford.

They descended slowly. The staircase was long and shallow with a wide landing halfway down. Here a window whose crimson velvet curtains matched the Etoile de Hollande roses in a copper bowl on its sill, gave on to the garden. The wind was still fresh and skittish, sending the hedges rippling like green rivers.

'There's a candidate for the third side of our triangle,' said Wexford, pointing down at the hothouse.

'Sean Lovell?' Burden's intense disapproval of this suggestion, with all its attendant implications, showed in an angry frown. 'The gardener's boy? Why, he can't be more than twenty and she . . . I never heard of such a thing!'

'Oh, rubbish,' said Wexford. 'Of course you've heard of it. Even you must have heard of Lady Chatterley, if you haven't read it.'

'Well, a book,' said Burden, relieved that the chief inspector had chosen a literary rather than a real-life instance of what he considered a monstrous perversion 'Cold in here, isn't it? I suppose it must be the wind.'

'We'll go and have a warm in the hothouse.'

Sean Lovell opened the door for them and they stepped into steamy tropical heat. Pale orchids, green and lemony pink, hung from the roof in moss-lined baskets, and on the shelves stood cacti with succulent lily-shaped flowers. Scented steam had condensed on the cold glass and there was a constant soft dripping sound.

The perfume, the heat and the colours suited Sean's rather exotic looks. Although probably an inheritance from gypsy forbears, his jet-black hair and golden skin suggested Italian or Greek descent. Instead of jeans and sweater he should have worn a corsair's shirt and breeches, Wexford thought, with a red scarf round his head and gold hoops in his ears.

'She was a nice lady, a real lady,' Sean said gruffly. Viciously he snapped a fat leaf from a xygocactus

40

'Always on the look-out for what she could do for you. And she has to go and get herself murdered. It's like what my old lady says, it's always the good as dies young.'

'Mrs Nightingale wasn't that young, Lovell.'

A brilliant seeping of colour came into the olive-gold cheeks. ' 'Bout thirty, that's all she was.' He bit his lip. 'You can't call that old.'

Wexford let it pass. Elizabeth Nightingale had tried so hard with her creams and her muscle bracer that it seemed ungenerous, now that she was dead, to disillusion her admirers.

'I'd like to know your movements last night. What time d'you knock off here and where did you go?'

Sean said sullenly, 'I knock off at five. I went home to my tea. I live alone in the village with my old lady. I had my tea and I watched telly all evening.'

'Don't you have a girl friend?'

Instead of answering directly, Sean said, 'You seen the girls round here?' He gave Wexford a shifty look that gave him the appearance of a Greek pirate. 'Some evenings I watch telly and some I go into town and play the juke box at the Carousel. What else is there to do in a dump like this?'

'Don't ask me, Lovell. I'm asking the questions. You watched television right up to the time you went to bed?'

'That's what I did. Never went out again. You can ask my old lady.'

'Tell me what programmes you saw.'

'There was Pop Panel, then the Hollywood musical till ten.'

'You went to bed at ten?'

'I don't remember. I can't remember what I saw and when I went to bed. How can I? I reckon we went on with our viewing after that. Yeah, it was Sammy Davis

41

Junior, that's what it was.' The dark face lit suddenly with an almost religious awe. 'My God, I'd like to be like him. I'd like to *be* him.' Chilled by Wexford's eyes, he shifted his own and said rapidly, 'I've got to go now. I've got to get on with my work. Old Will'll be after me.'

He sidled past Wexford, roughly bruising cactus spikes as he made his escape. Suddenly in the doorway Mrs Cantrip loomed.

'Your dinner's ready in the kitchen, Sean. I've been looking all over for you. Get cracking, do, or it'll be stone cold.' Thankfully Sean marched out of the hothouse and, when no one called him back, made for the kitchen at a run.

'Odd, that,' said Wexford. 'Sammy Davis was booked to appear on television last night, but the programme was cancelled at the last moment. They put on an old film instead.' He patted Burden's shoulder. 'Off you go to lunch now, Mike. I'll join you when I can.'

He watched Burden go, and then, almost running himself, he caught up with Mrs Cantrip. 'Is there anyone else living in this house or employed here that I haven't yet seen?'

'No, sir.' Her look told him that she was still bemused with shock, the reins of the household as yet unsteady in her hands. 'Would you be wanting a bite to eat?' she asked tremulously. 'You and the other police gentlemen?'

'No, thank you.' Wexford put a firm hand under her elbow as she tripped at the terrace steps. 'You can tell me one thing, though. Who were Mrs Nightingale's friends? Who came visiting to the Manor?'

She seemed pleased at this tribute to her dignity as a valued and confidential servant. 'Mrs Nightingale was never one of them as gossips, sir, or passes the day on the telephone. The ladies she saw was to do with business, like, arranging bazaars and gymkhanas, if you know what I mean. Then . . .' Her voice took on a sad importance, 'Then there was *their* friends as came here to dine, Sir George and Lady Larkin-Smith, and Mr and Mrs Primero, and all the county folks, sir.'

'Gentlemen friends? Please don't be offended, Mrs Cantrip. These days a lady can have men friends without there being anything—er, wrong.'

Mrs Cantrip shook her head vigorously. 'Her friends was their friends, sir,' she said, adding with a shade of sarcasm, 'Would there be anything else you wanted to know?'

'There is just one thing. A question of laundry. Whose job is it to change the linen in this house, the—er, sheets and towels?'

'Mine, sir,' said Mrs Cantrip, surprised.

'And did you remove any damp towels from Mr Nightingale's bedroom this morning?'

'No, sir, definitely not. I wasn't looking for work this morning and that's a fact.' Mrs Cantrip gave a virtuous lift of her chin. 'Besides, it's not the day for that,' she said. 'I change the sheets Monday mornings, and the towels Mondays and Thursdays. Always have done, year in and year out since I've been here.'

'Suppose someone else were to have . . . ?' Wexford began carefully.

'They couldn't have,' said Mrs Cantrip sharply. 'The soiled linen's kept in a bin in the back kitchen and no one's been near it today. I can vouch for that. Now, if you'll excuse me, sir, I've got my lunch to serve. I'm sure I don't know if Mr Nightingale's feeling up to a snack but there's the tray to go over to Mr Villiers as usual . . . Oh, my dear God! Mr Villiers! I'd forgot all about Mr Villiers.'

Wexford stared at her. 'D'you mean to say Mr

Nightingale's brother-in-law lives in this house?'

'Not to say "lives", sir,' said Mrs Cantrip, still wide-eyed, a red hand frozen to her cheek. 'He comes up every day to do his writing in the Old House. And, oh, sir, I don't reckon no one's told him!'

'Mr Villiers must have seen all our comings and goings.

'He wouldn't, sir. You can't see a thing from the Old House on account of all them trees, no more than you can see *it* from the outside. I'll have to go and tell him. All I can say is, thank God they wasn't close. He won't take it hard, there's one blessing.'

She trotted off at a half-run. Wexford watched her disappear under an arch in the hedge, an arch overhung with the leaves of lime trees turning gold. Above these all that showed of the Old House was a shallow roof against the white-spotted blue sky.

He allowed her five minutes and then he followed the path she had taken. It led him into a little paved court in the centre of which was a small square pond. Carp swam in the dark clear water under the flat shining rafts of lily leaves.

The court was heavily shaded by the trees which surrounded it. Their roots had sapped strength from the narrow borders, for nothing grew in them but a few attenuated and flowerless plants stretching desperately in the hope of reaching the sun. Mrs Cantrip must have entered the ancient house—to Wexford it appeared at least four hundred years old—by a black oak door which stood ajar. By the step stood a boot-scraper, a cock with spread wings made of black metal. Looking up past creeper-grown lattice windows, Wexford noticed its fellow, a crowing chanticleer on the weather vane.

As he entered the Old House, he became aware that the wind had dropped.

4

THE place in which Wexford found himself was evidently used as a storeroom. Birch logs were stacked against the walls in pyramids; racks above them awaited the Manor harvest of apples and pears. It was all very clean and orderly.

Since there was no other room down here and no sign of Denys Villiers' occupation, Wexford ascended the stairs. They were of black oak let into a kind of steeply sloping tunnel in the thick wall. From behind the single door at the top he heard low voices. He knocked. Mrs Cantrip opened the door a crack and whispered:

'I've broke the news. Will you be wanting me any more?'

'No, thank you, Mrs Cantrip.'

She came out, her face very red. A shaft of sunlight stabbed the shadows of the lower room as she let herself out. Wexford hesitated and then he went into Villiers' writing room.

The classics master remained sitting at his desk but he turned a grave cold face towards Wexford and said, 'Good morning, Chief Inspector. What can I do for you?'

'This is a bad business, Mr Villiers. I won't keep you long. Just a few questions, if you please.'

'Certainly. Won't you sit down?'

A large, somewhat chilly room, darkly panelled. The windows were small and obscured by clustering leaves.

There was a square of carpet on the floor. The furniture, a horsehair sofa, two Victorian armchairs with leather seats, a gateleg table, had apparently been rejected from the Manor proper. Villiers' desk was a mass of papers, open works of reference, tins of paper clips, ballpoint pens and empty cigarette packets. At one end stood a stack of new books, all identical to each other and to the one Wexford had seen on Nightingale's bedside table: *Wordsworth in Love*, by Denys Villiers, author of *Wordsworth at Grasmere* and *Anything to Show More Fair*.

Before sitting down, Wexford picked up the topmost of these books just as he had picked up the one in the bedroom, but this time, instead of quickly scanning the text, he turned it over to eye the portrait of Villiers on the back of its jacket. It was a flattering photograph or else taken long ago.

The man who faced him, coldly watching this brief perusal, seemed in his late forties. He had once, Wexford thought, been fair and handsome, strikingly like his dead sister, but time or perhaps illness had taken all that away. Yes, illness probably. Men dying of cancer looked like Villiers. In their faces Wexford had seen that same dusty parched look, yellowish-grey drawn features, blue eyes bleached a haggard grey. He was painfully thin, his mouth bloodless.

'I realise this must have been a great shock to you,' Wexford began. 'It seems unfortunate that no one broke the news to you earlier.'

Villiers' thin colourless eyebrows rose a fraction. His expression was unpleasant, supercilious. 'Frankly,' he said, 'it makes very little difference. My sister and I weren't particularly attached to each other.'

'May I ask why not?'

'You may and I've no objection to answering you. The

46

reason was that we had nothing in common. My sister was an empty-headed frivolous woman and I—well, I am not an empty-headed frivolous man.' Villiers glanced down at his typewriter. 'Still, I hardly think it would be tactful for me to do any more work today, do you?'

'I believe you and your wife spent last evening at the Manor, Mr Villiers?'

'That is so. We played bridge. At ten-thirty we left, drove home and went to bed.' Villiers' voice was clipped and sharp with an edge of temper to it, a temper that could be quickly aroused. He coughed and pressed his hand to his chest. 'I have a bungalow near Clusterwell. It took me about ten minutes to drive there from the Manor last night. My wife and I went straight to bed.'

Very tidy and brief, thought Wexford. It might all have been rehearsed beforehand. 'How did your sister seem last night, sir? Normal? Or did she appear excited?'

Villiers sighed. More from boredom than sorrow, Wexford decided. 'She was just as she always was, Chief Inspector, the gracious lady of the Manor whom everyone loved. Her bridge was always appalling, and last night it was neither more nor less appalling than usual.'

'You knew she went for nocturnal walks in the forest?'

'I knew she went for nocturnal walks in the *grounds*. Presumably it was because she was foolish enough to venture further that she met the end she did.'

'Is that why,' asked Wexford, 'you weren't surprised to hear of her death?'

'On the contrary, I was very surprised. Naturally, I was shocked. But now that I've considered it, no, I'm not very surprised any more. Women on their own in lonely places do get murdered. Or so I'm told. I never read the newspapers. Matters of that kind don't interest me.'

'You've certainly made it clear that you disliked your

sister.' Wexford glanced about the large quiet room. 'Strange, under the circumstances, that you should have been among those who accepted her bounty.'

'I accepted my brother-in-law's, Chief Inspector.' White with anger or with some other emotion Wexford couldn't analyse, Villiers sprang out of his chair. 'Good morning to you.' He opened the door and the dark stair well yawned ahead of him.

Wexford got up to leave. Halfway across the room he stopped and looked at Villiers, suddenly puzzled. It was impossible to believe the man could look worse, more ill, more corpselike, than when he had first seen him. But now as he stood in the doorway, one thin arm outflung, all vestige of colour, yellow-greyish pigment as it was, had drained from his skin.

Alarmed, Wexford started forward. Villiers gave a strange little gasp and fainted into his arms.

'Here we are, then,' said Crocker, who was the police doctor and Wexford's friend. 'Elizabeth Nightingale was a well-nourished and extremely well-preserved woman of about forty.'

'Forty-one,' said Wexford, taking off his raincoat and hanging it on the peg behind his office door. A couple of rounds of beef sandwiches and a flask of coffee, sent down from the canteen, awaited him on the corner of his desk. He sat down in the big swivel chair and, after looking distastefully at the topmost sandwich which was beginning to curl at the edges, started on it with a sigh.

'Death,' said the doctor, 'resulted from a fractured skull and multiple injuries to the brain. At least a dozen blows were struck by a not very blunt metal instrument. I don't mean an axe or a knife, but something with sharper edges to it, for instance, than a lead pipe or a poker. Death occurred—well, you know how hard it is to estimate—say after eleven p.m. and before one a.m.'

Burden was sitting against the wall. Above his head hung the official map of the Kingsmarkham district on which the dark mass of Cheriton Forest showed like the silhouette of a crouching cat. 'Nothing's come of our search of the grounds and the forest so far,' he said. 'What sort of a weapon had you in mind?'

'Not my job, Mike old boy,' said Crocker, moving to the window and staring down at the High Street below. Possibly he found this familiar sight boring, for he breathed heavily on the pane and began to draw on the breath film a pattern that might have been a pot plant or a diagram of the human respiratory system. 'I just wouldn't have a clue. Could be a metal vase or even a cooking utensil. Or a fancy ashtray or fire-tongs or a tankard.'

'You think?' said Wexford, munching scornfully. 'A fellow goes into a wood to murder a woman armed with an egg-whisk, does he, or a saucepan? A bloke sees his wife carrying on with another man so he whips out the carved silver vase he happens to have in his pocket and bops her over the head with it?'

'You don't mean to say,' said the doctor, shocked, 'that you've got that pillar of society Quentin Nightingale lined up for this job?'

'He's human, isn't he? He has his passions. Frankly, I'd rather plump for that brother of hers, that Villiers. Only he looks too ill to lift a knife and fork, let alone hit anyone with a frying pan.' Wexford finished his sandwiches and replaced the cap on the thermos flask. Then he swivelled round and gazed thoughtfully at the doctor. 'I've been talking to Villiers,' he said. 'He impressed me as a very sick man, among other things. Yellow skin, trembling hands, the lot. Just now, when I was leaving, he fainted dead away. For a minute I thought he was dead, but he came to all right and I got him over to the Manor.'

'He's a patient of mine,' said Crocker, rubbing out his drawing with the heel of his hand and revealing to Wexford his favourite view of ancient housetops and old Sussex trees. 'The Nightingales go privately to some big nob but Villiers has been on my list for years.'

'And you,' said Wexford sardonically, 'being a true priest of the medical confessional, are going to keep whatever's wrong with him locked up in your hippocratic bosom?'

'Well, I would if there was anything to lock. Only it so happens that he's as fit as you are.' Crocker eyed Wexford's bulk, the purple veins prominent on his forehead. 'Fitter,' he said critically.

With an effort Wexford drew in the muscles of his abdomen and sat up straighter. 'Ain't that amazement?' he said. 'I thought it was cancer, but it must be some inner torment feeding on his damask cheek. Like guilt. How old is he?'

'Now look . . .' said the doctor, fidgeting in his seat.

'Go on, strain yourself. A man's age isn't something he confides to his quack behind the aseptic green shades of the consulting room.'

'He's thirty-eight.'

'*Thirty-eight!* He looks ten years older and damn' ill with it. By God, Mike here is a stripling compared to him.'

Two sets of ageing eyes focussed speculatively on Burden, who looked modestly away, not without a certain air of preening himself. The doctor said rather pettishly, 'I don't know why you keep on about him looking ill. He works himself too hard, that's all. Anyway, he doesn't look that ill or that old.'

'He did today,' said Wexford.

'Shock,' said the doctor. 'What d'you expect when a man hears his sister's been murdered?'

'Just that, except that he evidently hated her guts. You should have heard the generous fraternal things he said about her. As nasty a piece of work as I've come across for a long time is Mr Villiers. Come on, Mike, we're going to call on some ladies who will melt and tell all under the effect of your sexy and—may I say?—youthful charm.'

They all went down together in the lift and the doctor left them at the station steps. The wind had dropped entirely but the High Street was still littered by the debris the gale had left in its wake, broken twigs, a tiny empty chaffinch nest blown from the crown of a tall tree, here and there a tile from an ancient roof.

Bryant drove them out of town by the Pomfret road, soon taking the left-hand fork for Myfleet. Their route led them past Kingsmarkham Boys' Grammar School, more properly known as the King Edward the Sixth Foundation for the Sons of Yeomen, Burgesses and Those of the Better Sort. The sons were at present home for the summer holidays and the brown-brick Tudor building bore a lonelier, more orderly, aspect than in term-time. A large new wing—a monstrosity, the reactionaries called it —had been added to the rear and the left side of the old school five years before, for the yeomen and burgesses, if not the better sort, had recently increased in alarming numbers.

The school had a dignity and grace about it, common to large buildings of its vintage, and most Kingsmarkham parents sought places there for their sons, setting aside with contempt the educational and environmental advantages of Stowerton Comprehensive. Who wanted a magnificent steel and glass science lab, a trampoline room or a swimming pool of Olympic standard, when they could instead boast to their acquaintance of historic portals and worn stone steps trodden (though on one single occasion) by the feet of Henry the Eighth's son? Besides, if your boy was at what everyone called the 'King's' school you could quite convincingly pretend to those not in the know that he attended a public school and conceal the fact that the State paid.

Burden, whose son had been admitted there one year before on passing a complex and subtle equivalent of the Eleven-plus, now said:

'That's where Villiers teaches.'

'Latin and Greek are his subjects, aren't they?'

Burden nodded. 'He takes John for Latin. I reckon he teaches Greek to the older ones. John says he works there a lot after school hours, doing something in the library. That's the library there in the new wing.'

'Research for his books?'

'Well, it's a marvellous library. Not that I know much about these things, but I went round it on Open Day and it impressed me no end.'

'John like him, does he?'

'You know what these boys are, sir,' said Burden. 'Those little devils in John's class call him Old Roman Villa. Good disciplinarian, I'd say.' And the father who had that morning mollified his own son with a gratuitous half-crown added severely: 'You have to be tough when you're dealing with these young lads, if you ask me.'

Grinning to himself, Wexford changed the subject. 'There are three main questions I'd like the answers to,' he said. 'Why was Quentin Nightingale taking a bath at five in the morning? Or, conversely, why does he pretend he was? Why did Sean Lovell tell me he was watching a

52

programme on the television last night that was, in fact, cancelled at the last moment? Why did Elizabeth Nightingale get on well with everyone except her only brother?'

'Why, for that matter, sir, did she have no intimate friends?'

'Perhaps she did. We shall have to find out. Mike, we're coming into Clusterwell. D'you happen to know which belongs to Villiers?'

Burden sat up straighter and turned his eyes to the window. 'It's outside the village, on the Myfleet side. Not yet, wait a minute. . . . Slow down, will you, Bryant? That's it, sir, standing by itself.'

Frowning a little, Wexford scanned the isolated bungalow. It was a squat, double-fronted place with two low gables under which were bay windows.

'Needs a coat of paint,' said Burden, contrasting it unfavourably with his own attractive, soon to be completely redecorated home. 'Shabby-looking dump. You'd think he could afford a decent garage.'

The front garden was a mass of Michaelmas daisies, all one colour. At one side a long drive of cracked and pitted concrete led to a prefabricated asbestos garage with a roof of tarred felt.

A black Morris Minor stood on this drive just in front of the asbestos doors and someone had very recently cleaned it, for there were damp patches on its bodywork and a small pool of water lay in a pothole under its rear bumper.

'That's odd,' said Wexford. 'Your sister is murdered, you pass out when you hear the news, and yet a couple of hours later you're lively enough to give your car a wash and brush-up.'

'It isn't his car,' Burden objected. 'He drives an Anglia. That belongs to his wife.'

'Where's his, then?'

'Still up at the Manor, I suppose, or in that revolting apology for a garage.'

'I wouldn't have said it was muddy in the forest last night, would you?'

'Tacky,' said Burden. 'We had rain at the weekend if you remember.'

'Drive on, Bryant. We'll leave the Villiers in undisturbed domestic bliss a little longer.'

The first person they saw when they parked in Myfleet village was Katje Doorn, coming out of the general store with a bag of fruit and a bottle of shampoo. She giggled happily at them.

'Do you happen to know which is the Lovells' cottage, Miss Doorn?' Burden asked her stiffly.

'Yes, look, it is that one.' She pointed, clutching the cringing inspector's arm and, as Wexford put it later, almost engulfing him in delectable curves. 'The most dirty in all the village.' As representative of perhaps the most house-proud nation on earth, she shuddered and, for the first time in their short acquaintance, lost her amiable expression. 'They are living there like pigs, I think. His mother is a very nasty dirty woman, all fat.' And, some six inches from her own rich contours, she described in the air a huge cello shape.

Wexford smiled at her. 'Will the fat lady be at home, do you know?'

Katje ignored the smile. She was looking at Burden. 'Maybe,' she said, shrugging. 'I know nothing of what these pig people do. You are liking a nice cup of tea? I think you are working very hard and would like some tea with me while your chief is in the nasty dirty cottage.'

'Oh, no—no, thank you,' said Burden, appalled.

'Perhaps tomorrow, then,' said Katje, sucking her hair. 'All evenings I am free and tomorrow my friend must work late, serving drinks for the dance. Mind you are not forgetting.' She wagged her finger at him. 'Now I say good-bye. Do not be catching anything nasty in that very dirty place.'

She tripped, straight-backed, yellow hair bobbing, across the road and up to the Manor gate. There she stopped and waved to them, her round breasts rising under the pink fluffy sweater.

Wexford waved back, turned away, laughing. 'Odds my little life, I think she means to tangle your eyes too!'

'A ghastly young female,' said Burden coldly.

'I think she's charming.'

'Good heavens, if I thought my daughter . . . !'

'For God's sake, Mike. I'm a married man, too, and a faithful husband.' His grin dying now, Wexford patted his large belly. 'Don't have much chance to be otherwise, do I? But sometimes . . .' He sighed. 'God, what wouldn't I give to be thirty again! Don't look at me like that, you cold fish. Here we are at this very nasty dirty place and let's hope we catch nothing more from our afternoon's work than a *nostalgie de boue.*'

'A what?' said Burden, trying to open the front gate without getting his hand stung by the nettles that thrust their leaves through it.

'It is just,' said Wexford with a rueful smile, 'a long name for a kind of chronic plague.' He laughed at Burden's incredulous suspicious face. 'Don't worry, Mike, it's not infectious and it only attacks the old.'

5

Not only the front gate, but the front door too, was overgrown with nettles and their antidote, the dock. Before they had a chance to lift the knocker a grey lace curtain, re-perforated with larger holes, was lifted at a lattice window and a face appeared.

'I don't know what you want but you'll have to go round the back.'

The side gate fell over as they pushed it. With a shrug, Wexford laid it down flat on a luxuriant bed of weeds. The back garden was a squalid blot on a fair landscape, the magnificence of the forest showing up, like a stain on black velvet, these twenty square yards of waist-high grass, dandelions, tumbled corrugated iron and broken chicken coops. A reasonably shipshape shed filled one of the farthest corners, its footings hidden under heaps of rags, green glass bottles and a mattress which looked as if it had been used for bayonet practice. Among the weeds an enamel chamber-pot and several battered saucepans could be discerned. Wexford noticed that a gate in the back fence led directly into the forest.

The back door opened suddenly and the woman who had spoken to them from the window put her head out.

'What d'you want?'

'Mrs Lovell?'

'That's right. What d'you *want*?'

'A word with you, if you please,' Wexford said smoothly. 'We're police officers.'

She gave them a narrow suspicious glance. 'About her over at the house, is it? You'd better come in. His lordship said there was police about.'

'His lordship?' queried Burden. Had the exalted circles in which they found themselves even more exalted people, in fact titled personages, on their perimeters?

'My son, my Sean,' said Mrs Lovell, disillusioning him. 'Come on. You can go in the lounge, if you like. In here.'

This room, euphemistically named, was slightly less dirty than the kitchen, but it too smelt of greens, a chronic gas leak, faintly of gin. It was furnished with a new bright pink suite, already soiled, and a heterogeneous assortment of ancient cottage pieces and modern gimcrack. The Queen smiled aloofly from a calendar, pinned to the wall between newspaper cut-outs of the Rolling Stones and a large framed oil of a Roman lady stabbing herself.

In feature she wasn't unlike Mrs Lovell, while unable to compare with her in amplitude. There was a strong flavour of the gypsy in Mrs Lovell's still-handsome face, the aquiline nose, full curved lips and black eyes. Medusa hair, black and tangled, fell to her shoulders. Her embonpoint didn't extend to her face. The impression was that fat had crept upwards to cease at the neck, deterred perhaps by the threat implicit in that strong unwrinkled chin.

Her body was enormous, but not without a coarse attraction, the fat distributed hugely in the right places. The bosom of a Mother Earth goddess, sixty inches round yet discernibly cloven, matched in girth immense hips. Like Katje, Mrs Lovell lacked inhibition and when she sat down her already low-cut blouse strained a further two inches down, corresponding to the ascent above her knees of a tight black skirt. Feeling that where feminine flesh was concerned, enough was enough for one afternoon—

besides, in this case, the flesh could have done with a bath
—Wexford looked away.

'We're just making routine enquiries, Mrs Lovell,' he
said. 'Would you mind telling me how your son spent last
evening?'

'Had his tea,' she said. 'Then he sat about watching the
TV. His lordship's keen on the TV, and why not, being
as he pays the licence?'

'Why not indeed? But he didn't watch it after nine-
thirty, did he?'

Mrs Lovell looked from Wexford to Burden. It was
transparent she was deciding whether to lie or tell the
truth, perhaps only because telling the truth is always
easier. Everything about her appearance and that of the
cottage testified to a gross laziness, a deadly sloth. At last
she said economically, 'He went out.'

'Where did he go?'

'I never asked him. I don't interfere with his ways . . .'
She picked at a ragged thumbnail. '. . . and he don't with
mine. Never have. Maybe he went down the shed. Spends
a lot of time down the shed, he does.'

'Doing what, Mrs Lovell?'

'His lordship's got his records down there.'

'Surely he can play his records in the house?' said
Burden.

'Can if he wants.' Mrs Lovell chewed a hangnail. 'Don't
matter to me one way or another. I don't interfere with
him and he don't with me.'

'What time did he come in?'

'I never heard him. My gentleman friend come in about
seven. Sean and him, they don't hit it off all that grand.
I reckon that was why his lordship took himself off down
the shed. He hadn't come in when my friend went, half

ten that'd have been—but there, like I say, I don't interfere with him and he don't . . .'

'Yes, yes, I see. Sean was very fond of Mrs Nightingale,
I believe?'

'You can believe what you like.' Mrs Lovell gave a huge
yawn, revealing fine sharp teeth. 'Live and let live, that's
my motto. Her up at the Manor, she believed in interfering with folks, making them better themselves. Gave
his lordship some funny ideas.' She stretched her arms
above her head, yawned again and swung her legs up on
to the sofa. Wexford thought of a fat cushiony cat, purr-
ing and preening itself, unconscious of the squalor in
which it lived.

'What sort of ideas?' he asked.

' 'Bout getting into show business, singing, all that. I
never took no notice. Maybe she fancied him. I never
asked.'

'Would you have any objection if we searched this
house?'

For the first time she smiled, showing an unsuspected
ironic humour. 'Search all you like,' she said. 'Rather you
than me.'

'A depressing experience,' said Wexford as they
returned to the car. Bryant, rather pale, followed at a
distance.

'Never in all my years of C.I.D. work have I come
across anything like it,' Burden exploded. 'I itch all over.'
He wriggled inside his clothes, scratching his head.

'Well, your young lady friend did warn you.'

Burden ignored this. 'Those beds!' he said. 'That
kitchen!'

'More than I'd bargained for, I admit,' Wexford agreed.
'The only clean place was that shed. Odd that, Mike. A

rug on the floor, couple of decent chairs, a record-player. Could be a love-nest.'

Burden shuddered. 'No one's ever going to make me believe a lady like Mrs Nightingale would have assignations there.'

'Perhaps not,' Wexford said reluctantly. 'On the practical side, we didn't unearth much, did we? One brass candlestick and a metal hot-water bottle. They hadn't got blood on them and they hadn't been cleaned, by God, in the last fifty years. And the clothes she said "his lordship" wore last night were almost natty. But what was he doing, Mike? Bryant checked on the pub and he wasn't there. The last bus out of Myfleet goes at nine-twenty, so he wasn't on that. A boy like Sean Lovell doesn't traipse about admiring the beauties of nature. He gets too much of that all day long.'

'Nobody,' Burden persisted doggedly, 'is going to make me believe there was anything between him and Mrs Nightingale. That mother of his is no more than the village trollop, if you ask me. "I don't interfere with him" indeed. That's just another way of saying you've always neglected your child. I know you think I'm old-fashioned, sir, and a puritan, but I don't know what women are coming to these days. Dirty, feckless or immoral, or the whole lot together. First there's this Mrs Nightingale with her face-lifting and her secret meetings, then there's that Dutch girl boasting of the way she carries on, and as for Mrs Lovell . . .'

'I thought you'd feel that way,' said Wexford with a kindly smile, 'and that's why I'm laying on something respectable for you. We are going to call on a virtuous wife, Mrs Georgina Villiers, who will tell us, I hope, without fainting or assuring us of her broken-hearted devotion to Mrs Nightingale's memory, just who her friends were and what her nasty brother did to make them loathe each other.'

'My husband's gone back to the Manor,' said Georgina Villiers. 'He won't be long.'

'We should like to talk to you.'

'Oh, would you?' Mrs Villiers looked surprised and rather frightened, as if few people had ever wanted to talk exclusively to her. 'Well, all right.'

She led them by way of a porridge-papered hall into a porridge-papered living room. It was as untidy and characterless as its owner, who stood awkwardly before saying in the abrupt voice of a charmless woman, 'Well, sit down.'

'We shan't keep you long, Mrs Villiers. How is your husband after this morning's shock?'

'Oh, that. He's all right now.' Suddenly she became aware that her visitors wouldn't sit down before she did and, with a slight nervous laugh, she crossed the room and perched herself on the arm of a chair. 'Oh, dear. I'd better close the front door. Excuse me, I'll just do that.' Wexford noticed that for so thin and slight a woman she had a strong athletic stride. Her legs, stockingless, were well muscled, tanned a reddish brown.

'Well, what did you want to ask me?' Her voice had a brusque barking note, as if she were used to command but not always to having her commands obeyed. Hundreds of dark brown freckles peppered her skin, the white vulnerable skin of the auburn-haired. She seemed in her late twenties, a woman who didn't know how to make herself pretty but who tried. The edelweiss brooch on her blouse collar, the slide in her hair, showed that she tried. 'My husband—you really should talk to my husband. He won't be long.' She eyed the clock rather wildly. 'Quen—

my brother-in-law, that is—wouldn't keep him long. Anyway, what did you want to ask me?'

'First of all, Mrs Villiers,' said Burden, 'did you and your husband come straight back here after your visit to the Manor last night?'

'Oh, yes.'

'What did you do when you got home?'

'We went to bed. We both went straight to bed.'

'You had been driving the car I saw outside?' Wexford put in.

Georgina Villers shook her head so violently that her hair flew out, disclosing unsuitable pendant ear-rings. 'We went in Denys's car. We've got two cars. When we got married last year I had a car and he had a car. Only old cars, but we kept them both. They aren't worth much, you see.' She managed a feverish, very bright smile. 'He's out in his car now.'

'And yours, I see,' said Wexford in a pleasant fatherly voice, 'has just been cleaned. Always clean your car on a Wednesday, do you, Mrs Villiers? I expect you're like my wife, a special time of the week for every little chore, eh? That way nothing gets left.'

'No, I'm afraid not. I'm not methodical.' She blinked at him, puzzled by the turn the conversation had taken. 'I ought to be, I know. Denys would like it if . . . Why do you ask?'

'I'll tell you, Mrs Villiers. If you were very methodical and always worked to a routine you'd be conditioned to it, and then I could understand that even the violent death of your sister-in-law might not make you deviate from that routine. But since you aren't methodical and only, I assume, clean your car when you feel like it or when it needs it, why did you choose today of all days?'

She blushed deeply. A fear that was almost anguish

howed in her eyes and she blinked again, bringing her
hands together and then clasping them. 'I don't know
what you mean. I don't understand.'

'Don't distress yourself. Perhaps you cleaned the car
because you were upset. Was that it?' She was very slow
on the uptake, Wexford thought, too frightened or too
obtuse to see the loophole he was offering her. He offered
it more explicitly. 'I suppose you took the very sensible
attitude that when one is unhappy or worried, work is
the best thing to take one's mind off one's troubles?'

Relieved at last, she nodded. 'Yes, that was it.' Immediately she undid the small good her agreement had done
her. 'I wasn't very upset, not really. I mean, she wasn't
my sister.'

'That's true,' said Wexford. He drew his chair closer
towards her and their eyes met, hers held by his like the
eyes of a rabbit mesmerised by headlights. Suddenly
Burden was excluded and the two of them were alone.
'She was your husband's sister, of course, just a sister-in-
law.' Her face sharpened and hardened. 'They didn't like
each other much, did they?'

'No, they didn't.' She hesitated very briefly, sliding as
if involuntarily from the arm to the seat of the chair, but
not taking her eyes from Wexford's face. 'They didn't get
on at all,' she said. 'If you must know, Denys couldn't
stand her.'

'Strange, Mrs Nightingale seemed to get on with everyone else.'

'Did she? Oh, with the county people, you mean.' She
gave a deep quiet sigh and then spoke in a level rapid
voice, 'Elizabeth didn't have any real friends. My husband, he thinks she was killed by a maniac, one of those
men who attack women. I expect that's what it was. She

63

must have been mad, going into the forest at night. Really she was asking for it.'

'Perhaps,' Wexford said. He smiled genially to help the atmosphere relax. Georgina Villiers was calmer now. She unclasped her hands and looked down at them, breathing shallowly. 'Do you know why your husband didn't get on with his sister?'

'Well, they hadn't anything in common.'

And what, Wexford asked himself, does a woman like you, dull and characterless and conventional, have in common with an intellectual like Villiers, a teacher of classics, an authority on Wordsworth?

'I suppose,' she said, 'he thought her rather silly and extravagant.'

'And was she, Mrs Villiers?'

'Well, she had a lot of money, didn't she? He hadn't any other reason for not liking her, if that's what you mean. She and Quen were very ordinary people really. Not the sort of people I've been used to, of course. I never associated with people like that before I was married.'

'You got on well with them?'

'Quen was always kind.' Georgina Villiers twisted her wedding ring, moving it up and down her finger. 'He liked me for my husband's sake, you see. He and my husband are *great* friends.' She looked down, nervously biting her lip. 'But I think he got to like me for myself. Anyway,' she said, suddenly shrill and cross, 'why should I care? A man's wife ought to come first. He ought to think more of her than of outsiders, not go and do his work in somebody else's house.'

'You felt that Mr Nightingale had too great an influence over your husband?'

'I don't care,' said Georgina, 'for any outside interference.' She pulled at the ear-rings, slightly releasing the

crew of one of them. 'I was a teacher of physical education,' she said proudly, 'before I was married, but I've
given it up for good. Don't you think a woman ought to
stay at home and look after her husband? That's best for
people like us, have a real home and family without too
much outside interest.'

Frowning at Burden who was nodding his head approv-
ingly, Wexford said, 'Would you object if we searched
his house?'

Georgina hesitated, then shook her head.

The bungalow had another reception room and two
bedrooms, the smaller of which was unfurnished and uncarpeted.

'I wonder what he does with his money?' Wexford
whispered. 'He's got a good job and he writes those books.'

Burden shrugged. 'Maybe he's extravagant like his
sister,' he said. 'He'll be different now. He's got a good
wife.'

'Oh, my God!'

Searching the sparsely filled cupboards, Burden said
stiffly, 'Well, I think it makes a nice change, talking to an
ordinary decent woman.'

'Perhaps she is ordinary and decent. She's dull enough,
God knows. There's nothing here, no blood, nothing that
could conceivably have been used as a weapon.' They
moved on into the kitchen where Wexford lifted the lid
of the old-fashioned coke boiler. 'Blazing away merrily,'
he said. 'They could have burnt practically anything on
here and she's had hours to do it in.'

Georgina was waiting for them in the living room, sit-
ing apathetically, staring at the wall.

'I can't think why my husband's so long. You'd think
that today he'd want to be here with me. You'd think . . .'
suddenly she froze, listening intently. 'Here he is now.'

She leapt from her chair and rushed into the hall, slam ming the door behind her. Listening with half an ear to the whispered conversation between husband and wife Burden said, 'She's certainly a mass of nerves. It's almos as if she expected us to find something. I wonder if . . .'

'Sssh!' said Wexford sharply.

Denys Villiers walked into the room, talking over hi shoulder to his wife. 'I can't be in two places at once Georgina. Quen's in a bad way. I left him with Lione Marriott.'

Burden's eyes met Wexford's. The chief inspector go up, his eyebrows raised in pleased astonishment.

'Did I hear you mention the name Lionel Marriott?'

'I expect so, if you were listening,' said Villiers rudely He still looked a good deal more than thirty-eight, bu less ill than in the Old House that morning. 'Why, d'yo know him?'

'He teaches,' said Wexford, 'at the same school as yo do. As a matter of fact, his nephew is married to my elde daughter.'

Villiers gave him an offensive glance. 'Remarkable,' h said, his tone clearly implying that Marriott, a culture person and colleague of his own, had distinctly lowere himself in being associated by marriage with the chie inspector's family.

Wexford swallowed his wrath. 'Is he a friend of you brother-in-law's?'

'He hangs about the Manor from time to time.' Cold Villiers disengaged his arm from his wife's grasp an slumped into an armchair. He closed his eyes in despair c perhaps simply exasperation. 'I want a drink,' he said and as Georgina hovered over him, her ear-rings bobbin; 'There's a half-bottle of gin somewhere. Go and find it will you?'

6

IT was a great piece of luck, Wexford thought as he
strolled down Kingsmarkham High Street at sunset,
that by serendipity he had lighted on one of Quentin
Nightingale's cronies and that the crony was Lionel
Marriott. Indeed, had he been allowed to select from all
his vast acquaintance in the town one single person to
enlighten him on the Nightingales' affairs, Marriott would
have been that one. But it had never crossed his mind to
connect Marriott with the Manor, although perhaps it
should have done, for what great house in the whole
neighbourhood was closed to him? What person with any
pretension to culture or taste wasn't on hob-nobbing
terms with him? Who but a recluse could deny familiar-
ity with Kingsmarkham's most hospitable citizen and
most fluent gossip?

Wexford had met him half a dozen times and this was
enough for Marriott to count him one of his intimates
and to avail himself of a rare privilege. Few people in
Kingsmarkham knew the chief inspector's Christian name
and still fewer used it. Marriott had done so since their
first meeting and required in exchange that Wexford
should call him Lionel.

His own life was an open book. You might not want to
turn its pages, but if you hung back, Marriott himself
turned them for you, as anxious to enlighten you as to
his own affairs as to those of his huge circle of friends.

He was about Wexford's own age, but spry and wiry and he had been married once to a dull little woman who had conveniently died just as Marriott's boredom with matrimony was reaching its zenith. Marriott always spoke of her as 'my poor wife' and told stories about her that were in very bad taste but at which you couldn't help laughing, for his narrative gift and art of skilful digression was such as to reveal the funny side of every aspect of the human predicament. Afterwards you salved your conscience with the thought that the lady was better dead than married to Marriott, who could never for long be attached to just one person and 'all the rest', as Shelley puts it, 'though fair and wise, commend to cold oblivion'.

For 'cold oblivion' or, at any rate, loneliness, seemed to be Marriott's great dread. Why else did he fill his house with people every night? Why else teach English litera- ture at the King's School by day when he had a private income, sufficient even for his needs, his generosity and his hospitality?

Since his wife's death he hadn't been celibate and each time Wexford had encountered him it had been in the company of one of a succession of attractive well-dressed women in their forties. Very probably, he thought, as he entered the High Street alley that led down to Marriott's house, the current companion would be there now arranging Marriott's flowers, listening to his anecdotes, preparing canapés for the inevitable ensuing cocktail party.

His house was at the end of a Georgian terrace of which all but this first one had been converted into shops or flats or storeplaces. By contrast to their sad and dilapi- dated appearance, his looked positively over-decorated with its brilliant white paint, renewed every two years, its jolly little window boxes on each sill, and the six curly balconies which sprouted on its façade.

Those not in the know would have supposed it to be owned by a spinster of independent means and a fussy inclination towards horticulture. Smiling to himself, Wexford climbed the steps to the front door, ducking his head to avoid catching it on a hanging basket full of Technicolor lobelias and fire-engine geraniums. For once the alley wasn't chock-a-block with the cars of Marriott's visitors. But it was early still, not yet seven o'clock.

It was Marriott himself who came to the door, natty in a red-velvet jacket and bootlace tie, a can of asparagus tips in one hand.

'Dear old boy, what a lovely surprise! I was only saying five minutes ago how miserable I was because you'd utterly deserted me, and here you are. The answer to a sinner's prayer. Wouldn't it be lovely, I was saying, if dear old Reg Wexford were to turn up tonight?'

Wexford belonged to the generation and social stratum that feels almost faint to hear Christian names on the lips of mere acquaintances and he winced, but even he couldn't deny that whatever Marriott's faults, no one could make you feel as welcome as he did.

'I was passing,' he said, 'and anyway I want to talk to you.'

'And I've been longing to talk to you, so that makes two of us. Come in, come in. Don't stand there. You'll stay for my party, won't you? Just a little celebration, a few old friends who are dying to meet the great chief inspector after all the lovely things I've told them about you.'

Wexford found himself swept into the hall, propelled towards Marriott's drawing room. 'What are you celebrating?' He took a deep breath and brought out the first name. 'What is there to celebrate, Lionel?'

69

'Perhaps "celebrate" was the wrong word, dear old boy.
This part is more in the nature of an "I, who am about t
die, salute you" gathering, if you take my meaning.' H
peered up into Wexford's face. 'I see you don't. Well, no
a busy man like you would hardly realise that this is th
last night of the holidays and it's back to the spotty devil
tomorrow.'

'Of course,' Wexford said. He remembered now tha
Marriott always gave an end-of-the-holidays party an
that he always referred to his pupils at the King's Schoc
as the 'spotty devils'. 'I won't stay, though. I'm afraid I'r
being a nuisance, interrupting you when you're preparin
for a party.'

'Not a bit! You don't know how overjoyed I am to se
you, but I see from your icy looks that you disapprove
Marriott threw out his short arms dramatically. 'Tell me
what have I done? What have I said?'

Entering the drawing room, Wexford saw a bar impro
vised in one corner, and through the arch that led int
the dining room, a table loaded with food, roast fowl:
cold joints, a whole salmon, arranged among carelessl
scattered white roses. 'I see,' he said, 'that I was wron
in supposing you to have been a close friend of Elizabet
Nightingale.'

Marriott's mobile face fell, becoming suddenly but pe
haps not sincerely, lugubrious. 'I know, I know. I shoul
be in mourning, sackcloth and ashes, no less. Believe m
Reg, I wear the ashes in my heart. But suppose I were t
put all these dear people off and fling the baked meats t
the Pomfret broiler-pig farm, what good would it do
Would it bring her back? Would it wipe one tear fror
Quentin's cheek?'

'I suppose not.'

'Dear Reg, I can't bear your censure. Let me give yo

70

drink. A whisky, a pernod, a champagne cocktail? And little slice of cold duck to go with it?'

Overwhelmed as usual, Wexford sat down. 'Just a small whisky, then, but nothing to eat.'

'I'm an outcast, I suppose. You won't eat my salt.' Marriott trotted towards the bar, shaking his head. He began pouring huge measures of Vat 69 into cut-glass tumblers. Wexford knew it would be useless to demur. He eyed the room with an inward grin. Although he knew many of the antiques were almost priceless, the chandeliers unique and the décor the envy of every person of taste in the town, Marriott's drawing room always suggested to him a mixture of the Wallace Collection and an Italian restaurant in the Old Brompton Road. The walls were covered by bottle-green paper embossed with emerald fur and hung with gilt-framed brothel mirrors. On every table stood an assortment of carriage clocks, snuff-boxes and useless little bits of Crown Derby. You would be afraid to move except that you knew that whatever damage you did Marriott would only smile and tell you it didn't matter at all, so much more precious was your company, including your clumsiness, than any inanimate object.

The clatter of heels from the kitchen region told him there was a third person in the house, and as he took his triple whisky, the woman appeared carrying a tray loaded with more food. She was a tall blonde of about forty-five with charm bracelets on both wrists which rang like bells as she moved.

'This is Hypatia, my amanuensis,' said Marriott, seizing her arm. 'You've no idea the funny looks I get when I introduce her like that. But then people are so illiterate, aren't they? This is Chief Inspector Wexford, my dear, the guardian of our peace.'

71

Unmoved by Marriott's remarks, Hypatia extended large calm hand.

'She won't interfere with us,' said Marriott as if sh wasn't there. 'She's just going to have a bath and mak herself more beautiful than ever. Run along, Patty darling.'

'If you're sure that's enough nosh,' said Hypatia.

'Quite sure. We don't want any bilious attacks like la time, do we? Now then, Reg, do your grand inquisito stuff. I'm desolated that this isn't a social call, but I don delude myself.' Marriott raised his glass. 'Here's to kind ness!'

'Er—cheers,' said Wexford. He waited until the woma had gone and sounds had reached him of water gurglin through the pipes. Then he said, 'I want to know abou the Nightingales, anything you can tell me.' He grinne 'I know you won't let yourself be inhibited by any foolis scruples like good taste or not speaking ill of the dead.'

'I was very fond of Elizabeth,' said Marriott in a slightl offended tone. 'We'd known each other all our lives. W were infants together, in a manner of speaking.'

'A manner of stretching, more like,' said Wexfor nastily. 'She could have given you a good fifteen year: so don't kid yourself.'

Marriott sniffed. 'It's easy to see you got out of bed th wrong side this morning.'

'I don't know about the wrong side. I got out of it damn' sight too early. So you've known her since *she* wa born, have you? Where was that?'

'Here, of course. Didn't you know she and Denys wer born here?'

'I hardly know a thing about them.'

'Oh, that's what I like. Total ignorance. As I say to th spotty devils, blessed are they who hunger and thirst afte enlightenment, for they shall be filled, even if I have to knock it into 'em with a slipper. Well, they were born here all right, in a nasty little damp house down by Kingsbrook Lock. Their mother came from London, quite a good family, but their father was Kingsmarkham born and bred. He was a clerk in the council offices.'

'Not well-off, then?'

'Poor as church mice, my dear. Elizabeth and Denys went to the council school, as it then was, and no doubt he would have gone on wasting his sweetness on the desert air but for the bomb.'

'What bomb?' enquired Wexford as the bathroom door slammed and something went glug in the water tank far above their heads.

'One of that stick of bombs a German plane let fly over here on its way to the coast. It was a direct hit and it took Villiers *père* and *mère* to Kingdom Come in one fell swoop.'

'Where were the children?'

'Denys was out fishing and Elizabeth had been sent to fetch him home. It was early evening, about seven. The Villiers children, Elizabeth and Denys, were fourteen and eleven respectively.'

'What became of them?'

'A rather peculiar and most unfair arrangement was made for them,' said Marriott. 'Denys went to his mother's brother and did very well for himself. This uncle was a barrister in a good way of doing and he sent Denys to some public school and then to Oxford. Poor Elizabeth was left behind with her aunt, her father's sister, who took her away from the High School here when she was fifteen and sent her to work at Moran's, the draper's.'

Wexford's face registered the astonishment Marriott had hoped for. 'Mrs Nightingale a draper's assistant?'

'I thought that would shake you. That old bitch Priscilla Larkin-Smith still goes about telling her mates about the days when Elizabeth Villiers used to fit her for her corsets.'

'How did she meet Nightingale?'

'Oh, that was a long time later,' said Marriott. 'Elizabeth wasn't at Moran's for long. She ran away to London and got a job, the clever little thing. Have some more Scotch, ducky?'

'No, really. You know, Lionel, if it wasn't for What's-her-name upstairs and her predecessors, one would suspect you of—how shall I put it?—a certain ambivalence. Sometimes you're too epicene for words.'

Marriott smirked at that, not displeased. 'I do camp it up rather, don't I? People are always telling me about it. Just a pose, I assure you. Do let me fill your glass.'

'Oh, all right.' The water was running out of the bath now and Hypatia's feet could be heard tapping on the upper floor. 'Did the brother and sister meet in London?'

Marriott lit a Russian cigarette and blew elegant smoke rings. 'That I wouldn't know.' He looked crestfallen. Wexford knew he hated to admit ignorance of any detail of a friend's private life. 'I didn't see either of them again until I heard Quentin had bought the Manor.' He recharged their glasses and came back to his chair. 'When we heard the Manor had new people in I naturally got my wife to call. You can imagine my joy when I heard who this Mrs Nightingale was.'

'I'm not sure that I can,' said Wexford, 'seeing she was a kid of fifteen and you around thirty when you last met.'

'How you do throw cold water on all one's impulsive little expressions! I mean, of course, that it was lovely to see someone I used to know, and anyway it was always a pleasure to be with Elizabeth. An absolute beauty, you see, and what style! I love those classic English blondes.'

'You ought to get married again,' said Wexford.

Marriott cast a shifty glance upwards and said epigrammatically, 'A man who marries again doesn't deserve to lose his first wife.'

'Sometimes,' said Wexford, 'you shock me. Talking of marriage, how did the Nightingales get on?'

'They were a very happy couple. If you and your wife never discuss anything but the weather, are waited on hand and foot, are childless and equally cold sexually, what is there to quarrel about?'

'It was like that, was it? And may I ask how you know they were sexually cold?'

Marriott shifted a little in his seat. 'Well, you've only got to look at Quentin and . . . You must allow for a little guesswork, Reg.'

'I'll do the guessing. Let's get back to those early days, fifteen, sixteen years ago. Was Villiers living here then?'

'No, he turned up a couple of years later. First day of the autumn term it was, and that makes it fourteen years ago almost to the day. We had a couple of newcomers to the staff, a science man and a second-string classics bloke. That was Denys. The Head introduced us veterans and, of course, I was thrilled to see Denys.'

'But naturally,' said Wexford.

Marriott gave him an injured look. 'I thought his behaviour very odd, most peculiar. But then Denys is odd, the complete misanthropist. "What a stroke of luck for you," I said, "knowing me. I can take you around and introduce you to anyone who is anyone." You'd have thought he'd have been overjoyed, but not a bit of it. He just gave me one of his sick looks, but I thought I'd better make allowances.'

'Allowances for what?'

'Well, he's a poet, as you know, and poets are curious creatures. There's no getting away from it. I see you didn't know. Oh, dear me, yes. Several very charming little verses of his had appeared in the *New Statesman* by that time, and I'd just read his collection of essays on the Lake Poets. Most scholarly. So, as I say, I made allowances. "Perhaps you're relying on your sister to give you the entrée," I said. "Don't forget she's new here herself." "My sister here?" he said, going quite white. "You don't mean you didn't know?" I said. "Christ," he said, "I thought this was the last place she'd want to show her face in." '

'But you made sure they got together?' said Wexford.

'Naturally, my dear. I had Denys and his wife up there the same evening.'

'His *wife?*' Wexford almost shouted. 'But he's only been married a year.'

'No need to blow your cool, dear old boy. His first wife. You weren't joking when you said you didn't know anything about these people, were you? His first wife, June, a most . . .'

'Look, don't let's get on to her yet,' groaned Wexford. 'Why was Villiers so upset when you said his sister was here?'

'I asked myself the same thing at the time, but we were all together quite a lot after that and it was plain they couldn't stand each other. Odd when you think how sweet Elizabeth was to everyone else. Frankly, Reg, she acted towards him as if he'd done her some injury, and as for him . . . The man's rudeness to her was beyond belief. But you mustn't lay too much stress on that. Denys is foul to everyone except Quentin. He's quite different with Quen and, of course, Quen adores him. But Elizabeth and Denys were never friends. As children they were always quarrelling. Even now I can remember Mrs Villiers and my poor wife discussing it, how trying it was, you know, and how helpless it made Mrs Villiers feel. But if you want to know why they carried on with this feud of theirs, I can't help you. Elizabeth never discussed her brother if she could help it, and if she didn't confide in me, whom did she confide in? We were very close friends, intimate, you might say.'

'Might I?' said Wexford thoughtfully. 'Might I indeed?' He fixed Marriott with a searching look and would have pursued this further but for the entry of Hypatia, bathed, perfumed and dressed in gold trousers and a black and gold tunic.

She had a cool smile for Wexford, a maternal one for Marriott. 'Still nattering? Pam and Ian are here, Leo. I've just seen their car turn into the alley.'. She said pointedly to Wexford, 'Must you go?'

Wexford got up, shaking off Marriott's restraining hand. 'Will you be having another party tomorrow night, Lionel?'

'Really, Reg, I'm not a complete sybarite. Tomorrow night I'll be utterly prostrate after my tussles with the sons of yeomen, burgesses and those of the better sort. Spots before the eyes, no less.'

'In that case,' said Wexford, grinning, 'I'll pick you up from school and give you a lift home.'

'Lovely,' said Marriott, showing for the first time a vague uneasiness. He escorted Wexford to the door, let him out and admitted two bright elderly people. 'How marvellous to see you, my dears. You're looking good enough to eat, Pam darling. Now do let me . . .'

Wexford slipped quietly away.

7

THE Burden children were going back to school and from the bungalow bathroom came the sounds of retching. Pat was always sick on the first morning of term. Her parents stood in the kitchen listening to these sounds with the helpless misery of people who are just beginning to realise that their children are human beings as well as their children and that there is a point beyond which they cannot help them. This child would vomit on the first day of every term, before every interview for a job, probably too on her wedding morning.

'Oh, Mike,' said Jean Burden, 'ought we to send for Dr Crocker? Sometimes I even think about sending her to a psychiatrist.'

'When you know she'll be as right as rain as soon as she sets foot in the classroom? Keep a sense of proportion, love.'

'I just wish I could help her. We've never been nervy. I never thought I'd have a child who was a mass of nerves.'

'I'm not nervy,' said John, coming in with satchel and shining morning face. 'If I ever have kids and they go on like her I'll give them a right walloping.'

Burden looked at his son with distaste. His children, though only two years apart in age, brought up by loving and happily married parents in a solid middle-class background, had never got on. From quarrelling ever since

John was a toddler and Pat able only to scream at him from her pram they had progressed through physical fights to their current daily fripping.

He said severely: 'You're to stop speaking about your sister like that. I'm sick of telling you. Suppose,' he said, a thought coming to him from the case he was engaged on, 'suppose you and Pat were to be separated now and knew you wouldn't see each other again till you were grown up, how would you feel then? You'd be very sorry you were so unkind to her. You don't know how much you'd miss her.'

'I wouldn't miss her,' said John. 'I wish I was an only child.'

'I can't understand this dislike,' Burden said helplessly. 'It's not natural.' He put out his hand as his daughter, white-faced and with hanging head, came in under the shelter of her mother's arm. 'I'll drive you to school, sweetheart. I'll come right inside with you.'

'You never drive me to school,' said John. 'And I've got further to go, a dirty great mile to walk.'

'Don't say "dirty great",' said Burden mechanically, and then: 'I'll drive you both. But, for heaven's sake, don't quarrel in the car.'

The forecourt of the King's School was thronged with boys. Burden edged the car up the drive, sending the littlest ones, John's contemporaries, scuttling out of the way, squealing and whooping at the tops of their voices. Sixth-formers, draped against the wall in languid groups, their ignominious caps folded and tucked into their pockets, stared at him with lofty insolence. John jumped out of the car while it was still moving and was immediately absorbed by the whooping mob.

'You see, John isn't a bit worried,' Burden said encouragingly. 'You know you were both bored stiff being at home so long and he's glad to be back with his friends.'

'I hate him,' said Pat.

'That's no way to talk about your brother.' Burden reversed carefully and, making a three-point turn just inside the gates, came face to face with Denys Villiers. He nodded courteously, just raising his hand. Villiers looked through him, thrust his hands into his pockets, and marched in the direction of the new wing.

'Stop the car, Daddy,' Pat said as soon as they reached the open road. 'I'm going to be sick again.'

His children deposited, Burden drove down to the police station through the morning rush. He had been surprised to see Villiers, whom, he thought, tact if not grief would have kept from work for at least this week. A strange man, one who seemed to care nothing for public opinion. His behaviour in ignoring Burden, a policeman who had been in his house the day before and was, in any case, the parent of a King's pupil, had been—well, outrageous, Burden thought.

Aware that he was twenty minutes late, he leapt into the lift and arrived breathless in Wexford's office. The chief inspector, in an even more disgracefully shabby suit than usual, sat at his rosewood desk, leafing through stacks of papers. Standing behind him at the window was the doctor, breathing on the glass and drawing with one finger something that looked disturbingly like a plan of the alimentary canal. Burden had had enough of alimentary canals for one morning.

'Sorry I'm late,' he said. 'My girl Pat's always sick on the first day of term, so I hung about and drove her to school.' He nodded to the doctor. 'Jean wanted you called in.'

'But you wouldn't bother a busy man?' said Crocker

with a lazy grin. 'Pat'll grow out of it, you know. It's all part of the human predicament from which your kids aren't going to be absolved, hard cheese though that may be.'

Wexford looked up with a scowl. 'Spare us the philosophy, will you? I've got some lab reports here, Mike. The ash from the Manor bonfire shows distinctly that woollen cloth was burnt on it. No weapon has come to light, although our people went on combing the forest until it got dark last night and they're at it again now.'

'It could be anywhere,' Burden said hopelessly. 'In the river, chucked in someone's garden. We don't even know what it is.'

'No, but we're all going to have a hard think about that. First of all we have to decide if Mrs Nightingale's assailant planned this murder or if it was unpremeditated.'

Dr Crocker rubbed out his drawing with the heel of his hand. He sat down on one of Wexford's flimsy chairs. The chief inspector's was the only solid one in the room, a dark wood and leather throne, strong and ample enough to bear Wexford's weight. It creaked as Wexford leaned back, spreading his arms.

'Premeditated,' said the doctor, concentrating. 'Otherwise she wouldn't have been killed in that way in that place. The kind of thing she was killed with isn't the kind that people carry with them on country walks. Right?'

'You mean that if it was unpremeditated she could only have been killed by strangling, for instance?'

'Roughly speaking, yes. You don't have to bring the weapon with you in a planned murder if you know the means are going to be available. For example, Y intends to kill X in X's drawing room, but he doesn't take a weapon because he knows the poker will be where it always is, on the hearth. But in an open space there aren't going to be any means, so he arms himself before he starts. That's what your man did.'

'Does it have to be a man?' Wexford asked.

'A man or a very strong woman.'

'I agree with you. My own view is that it was planned, and that can still apply in a jealousy murder. The killer followed her, expecting to see what he did in fact see. He took the weapon with him, guessing what he was going to see and only waiting for confirmation. What do you think, Mike?'

'Unpremeditated,' said Burden coolly. 'Our murderer was carrying with him something that could be used as a murder weapon but had some other primary purpose. As in the case of a woman cutting bread. Her husband says something to her which drives her over the edge of reason and she makes for him with the bread knife. But the original purpose of having the knife in her hand was to cut bread.'

'I'm all for pre-cut loaves myself,' said the doctor facetiously.

A deepening frown was the only sign Wexford gave of having heard this. 'Well, if we play along for the moment with Mike's theory, what could he (or the very strong she) have been carrying? What do people carry when they go into a wood at night?'

'A walking stick,' said Burden promptly, 'with a metal tip.'

Crocker shook his head. 'Too thin. Not the kind of thing at all. A *shooting* stick possibly, but it seems far-fetched. A golf club?'

Wexford glared at him derisively. 'Going to have a few drives among the trees, was he? Trying to get his handi-cap down? Oh, give me strength!'

'Well, it was moonlight,' said the doctor. 'Or it was till the wind came up. Metal heel of a shoe?'

'Then where's the dirt in the wound?'

'You're right. There wasn't any.'

Wexford shrugged and fell into moody silence. Equally silently, Burden eased the papers from under his hand and began reading them without expression. Suddenly Wexford swivelled the groaning chair round.

'You said something just now, something about light.'

'I did?'

Burden said in his prim official voice: 'Dr Crocker said that it had been moonlight until the wind came up.' He gave a barrister-like inclination of his neat head in the doctor's direction. Crocker raised his eyebrows.

'Oh, yes. I remember because I was out at Flagford, delivering a baby. There was a bright moon but the clouds were already coming up by eleven and by half past the moon had gone.'

A slow grin that had nothing to do with humour and a great deal to do with triumph spread across Wexford's face. 'So what would anyone take with him into the wood?'

'An umbrella,' said the doctor, but Burden said, his gravity giving way to excitement, 'A torch!'

'A torch?' said Quentin Nightingale. 'Those we have are kept in the garden room.' The skin under his eyes looked brown and crêpey, the result perhaps of a second sleepless night. His hands trembled nervously as he touched his forehead, fidgeted with his tie, finally putting them behind his back and clasping them lightly together. 'If you think . . .' he muttered. 'If you're hoping . . . Your people searched the house throughout yesterday. What can . . . ?' He seemed incapable of ending his sentences, but let them trail away on a note of despair.

'I'm pursuing a new line,' Wexford said briskly. 'Where is this garden room?'

'I'll take you there.'

As they re-entered the hall the front-door bell rang. Quentin stared at the door as if Nemesis itself awaited him on the other side of it, but he made no move, only nodding limply when Mrs Cantrip marched out from the kitchen.

'Whoever's that now?' she said with some exasperation. 'Are you at home to visitors, sir?' His apathy aroused her sympathy rather than impatience. 'For two pins I'd send them away with a flea in their ear.'

'You'd better see who it is,' said Quentin.

It was Georgina Villiers and Lionel Marriott. They made a strange couple, the tall raw-boned young woman incongruously bedizened with costume jewellery, and the little sharp-eyed man. Georgina's face registered a mixture of assorted emotions, hope, shyness, an intense curiosity. She carried a canvas hold-all with plastic straps and handles, more suitable for a hiker than a woman paying a morning call, and as she stepped over the threshold she broke into a disjointed stream of apology and explanation.

'I felt I had to come and see how you were bearing up, Quen. It's all so dreadful for you. . . . I've brought my own lunch so that Mrs Cantrip won't have to be bothered cooking for me. How are you? You do look bad. Well, of course it's the strain and everything. Oh dear, perhaps I shouldn't have come.'

Quentin's face, contorted in an effort to hide his anxiety, showed plainly that he agreed with her, but courtesy forbade his saying so. 'No, no. It was nice of you to take the trouble. Won't you come into the morning oom?' He swallowed hard and half-turned to Wexford. Perhaps Mrs Cantrip can take you to where the torches re kept?' The hand he put up to his sister-in-law's shoulder to shepherd her along shook now with violent jerks hat were painful to see. They moved slowly towards the oom where Elizabeth Nightingale had sat in the mornings, Georgina still muttering apologies.

'One moment,' said Wexford, putting out an arm to prevent Marriott from following them. The morning-oom door closed. 'What the hell are you doing here, anyway?' the chief inspector said wrathfully. 'I thought you were supposed to be at school?'

'I had a free period, my dear, and how use it better than by popping up here to console poor Quen?'

'Perhaps you can tell me how someone without a car "pops", as you put it, up to Myfleet from Kingsmarkham and back again in forty minutes?'

'Georgina,' said Marriott, unable to restrain a grin of triumph, 'gave me a lift. I was standing at the school gates lost in thought, wondering in fact how I was going to accomplish my popping, the Myfleet bus having just gone, when along she came, Manor-bound. Such a relief! We had a nice little chat, planning the things we were going to say to cheer Quen up.'

'Then you'd better go in and say them,' said Wexford, giving the little man a small shove. 'Say them and go. I'm just about to start another massive search of this place and I don't want a lot of cheerful nosy people interfering with my men. And don't forget,' he added, 'that we have a date at four o'clock.' He sighed, shaking his head. 'Now, Mrs Cantrip, for the garden room.'

'Just down this passage, sir, and mind the step. I'm sure you'll say it was wrong of me to listen but I couldn't help hearing what you said to that Mr Marriott. Just what he

needs, I thought, always up here snooping. And as fo
that Mrs Villiers . . . Did you hear her say she'd brough
her own lunch? A nasty packet of sandwiches, I daresay
As if I wouldn't have given her a nice lunch. She'd onl
got to ask like a lady.'

'Is this the place, Mrs Cantrip? It's very dark dow
here.'

'You can't tell me, sir. I'm always telling Mr Nigh
ingale to have a light fixed up. There was quite a nast
accident five or six years back when that Twohey fe
down the step and thought his leg was broken but it wa
only a sprained ankle. He'd been too free helping himsel
from Mr Nightingale's whisky bottle and that's a fact.'

'Who was Twohey?' asked Wexford, stepping back fo
Mrs Cantrip to open the door. 'A friend of the family?'

'Oh, no, sir, just a servant. Him and his wife used t
work here, if you can call it work. It didn't lighten m
load, I can tell you. I was never so relieved in all my lif
as when Mr Nightingale sacked them. This is the garde
room, sir, and there's a bit more light, you'll be glad t
see.'

The light came from a glazed door leading into th
garden. His face impassive, Wexford looked slowly roun
the small uncarpeted room. Its walls were whitewashe
and on one of them hung a couple of shotguns, whil
beneath golf clubs and walking sticks lay in a long rack
There were two tennis rackets in presses, a string bag o
tennis balls and a chip basket and scissors for cuttin
flowers. His glance went up to a shelf above the rack o
which stood an array of torches: a lantern with a re
cone on its top of the kind that is used to warn motorist
of the presence of a broken-down car, a bigger storr
lantern, a pencil torch and a bicycle lamp.

'That's funny,' said Mrs Cantrip. 'There should b

another one, a great big silver-coloured one.' Suddenly she had become rather pale. 'A torch with a big head,' she said, 'a big head and a sort of long thick tube thing to hold it with. I reckon it'd be nine or ten inches long.'

'And it should be up there with the others?' Mrs Cantrip nodded, biting her lip. 'When did you last see it here?'

'Oh, it'd be two or three weeks back. You don't kind of clean a room like this, if you take my meaning, sir. There's like no dusting or polishing, you see. Young Sean gives it a sweep out every so often.'

'He does, does he?' Wexford pulled out from under the rack a short set of steps, mounted them and looked at the surface of the shelf. A thickish patina of dust lay on the unpainted wood. In the front, between the bicycle lamp and the storm lantern, was a dust-free circle some four inches in diameter.

He licked his finger and just touched the centre of this clean circle. Then he said, looking at his fingertip, 'That torch was taken down yesterday or the day before.' He wiped his finger on his handkerchief, observing that the linen was unmarked. His inspired guess had turned out to be well founded.

It was such a big house, he thought, as he emerged from the passage and stood once more in the hall, a big country house full of cupboards and hidey-holes. His men had been instructed to look for a weapon without being told what they should look for. Suppose they had seen the missing torch in Nightingale's bedroom, sticking out perhaps from the pocket of a raincoat, would any one of them have had the intelligence, the faculty of putting two and two together to make more than four, to note it and draw it to the attention of his superiors? Wexford

87

doubted it. They would have to begin again, this tim
with a specific missing object in view.

He tapped on the morning-room door, then opened i
There was no one inside. Only a cigarette end still smou
dering in a blue pottery ashtray showed that Marrio
had been there, then had obeyed Wexford and gone.

Giving himself *carte blanche* to explore the house a
he pleased, Wexford looked into the drawing room an
the dining room, and found both empty. He mounted th
stairs to the first landing, treading shed rose petals unde
foot, and peered out between the crimson velvet curtain
Georgina Villiers was standing on the lawn, munchin
sandwiches and talking to Will Palmer. There was n
sign of Quentin Nightingale. Wexford went down agai
entered the empty study and telephoned Burden, askin
him to come up to the Manor with Loring and Bryar
and Gates and anyone else he could get hold of. He pu
the receiver down and listened to the silence.

At first it seemed absolute. Then, from far above hin
he made out faintly thin reedy music from a transisto
Katje's perhaps; the tiny muted clink of plates as M
Cantrip prepared lunch; then footsteps coming from t
couldn't tell where but which brought Quentin Nigh
ingale into the room.

'A torch is missing from the garden room,' Wexfo
said in a cool level voice. 'A big torch, shaped like thi:
Using both hands, he drew it in the air. 'Have you see
it about lately?'

'It was there on Sunday. I went in to get my golf clu
and I noticed it was there.'

'It isn't there now. That torch killed your wife, N
Nightingale.'

Quentin leaned against a bookcase and put his head i
his hands. 'I don't honestly think,' he whispered, 'that

88

can take any more. Yesterday was the most ghastly day of my life.'

'I can understand that. I'm afraid I can't promise you today or tomorrow will be improvements.'

But Quentin seemed not to have heard him. 'I think I'm going mad,' he said. 'I must have been mad to do what I did. I'd give everything I've got to go back to Tuesday evening and start again.'

'Are you making me some sort of confession?' Wexford asked him sternly, getting up. 'Because, if so . . .'

'Not that sort of confession,' Quentin almost shouted. 'Something private, something . . .' He clenched his hands, threw up his head. 'Show me,' he said hoarsely, 'show me where you think this torch ought to be. I might be able . . . Just show me.'

'All right. I'll show you and then we'll have another little talk. But let me tell you one thing first. Nobody involved in a murder case has any private life. Please remember that.'

Quentin Nightingale made no reply, but he hunched his shoulders and again put that trembling hand to his forehead. Puzzled, Wexford speculated as to the nature of this acute anxiety that was turning the other man into a nervous wreck. Had he killed his wife? Or was this distress the result of some other act, something necessarily more venial, yet as productive of agonising guilt?

They walked down the dark passage, Wexford going first. Ahead of them a vertical slit of light showed the garden-room door slightly ajar.

'I closed that door,' Wexford said sharply and pushed it wide. On the high shelf where, half an hour before, there had been only a clean circular patch in the dust, stood a large chrome torch, up-ended.

8

THE torch had been scrubbed, probably immersed in water. Wexford held it gingerly in his handkerchief and unscrewed its base. The batteries had been removed but the glass and the bulb inside were unbroken. He noted that a few drops of water still clung to the interior of the tube that formed its handle.

Very slowly, he said, 'Only you, Mr Nightingale, knew that I came to this house this morning in search of a torch. Did you speak of it to any of your servants or to Mrs Villiers or Mr Marriott?'

White-faced, Quentin Nightingale shook his head.

'I believe,' Wexford said, 'that this torch was used to kill your wife. It wasn't here when I first visited the garden room; it is here now. Someone replaced it in the past half-hour. Come, let us go back to your study.'

The widower seemed unable to speak at all. He sank heavily into a chair and covered his face with his hands.

'Did you replace that torch, Mr Nightingale? Come, I want an answer. I shall sit here until I get one.' There was a tap at the door and Wexford opened it to admit Burden. A quick glance passed between them, Burden raised his eyebrows at the silent slumped figure, and then moved without speaking towards the wall shelves as if fascinated by the books they held. 'Pull yourself together, Mr Nightingale,' Wexford said. 'I'm waiting for an answer.' He would have liked to shake the man, stir him into some sort of response. 'Very well,' he said at last. 'Since I don't believe in wasting time and Inspector Burden looks as if he might appreciate a little entertainment, I'll tell you a story. You may find some parallels in it with your own conduct over the past days. Who knows?

'There was a country gentleman,' he began, 'who lived with his beautiful wife in a manor house. They were happy together, even if their marriage might have been said to have grown a little rusty and dull with the years.' Quentin moved a fraction at that, pushing his fingers hard into his white hair. 'One day,' Wexford said in the same pleasant conversational tone, 'he discovered that his wife was being unfaithful to him, meeting another man in the woods at night. So, consumed with jealousy, he followed her, taking a torch with him, for the moon had gone and the night was dark. He saw her with this man, kissing each other, and heard them making plans and giving promises. Perhaps they even abused him. When the man had left her and she was alone, the husband confronted her, she defied him, and he struck out at her with the torch, struck again and again in his jealous frenzy until he had beaten her to death. Did you say something, Mr Nightingale?'

Quentin's lips moved. He moistened them, struggled forward in his chair and managed a strangled, 'However . . . however it happened, it wasn't . . . it wasn't that way.'

'No? The husband didn't burn his bloodstained sweater on the still-smouldering bonfire? He didn't pace the garden for hours in his anguish, finally locking himself in his own bathroom to spend more hours cleansing every trace of his wife's blood from his person? Strange. We know he took a bath and that at what some would call an ungodly hour . . .'

'Stop!' Quentin cried, clutching the arms of his chair. 'None of this is true. It's a monstrous fabrication.' He swallowed, then cleared his throat. 'I didn't take a bath.'

'You told me you did,' retorted Wexford.

'Twice,' said Burden, the word dropping like a bead of cold water.

'I know. It was a lie.' A fiery blush coloured Quentin's face and he closed his eyes. 'Would you get me a drink, please? Whisky. It's in there.'

Burden looked at Wexford and Wexford nodded. The whisky was in a small cabinet under the window. Burden poured about an inch into a glass and put it into the shaking hand, closing the fingers around it. Quentin drank, the glass chattering against his teeth.

'I'll tell you where I was,' he said. Wexford noticed that he was at last making a determined effort to steady his voice. 'But you alone. I should like it if the inspector could leave us.'

And if he was about to confess to murder . . . ? Wexford didn't like it much. But he had to know. He made a quick decision. 'Will you wait outside, please, Inspector Burden?'

Obediently Burden went, without a backward glance. Quentin gave a heavy sigh. 'I don't know where to begin,' he said. 'I could just tell you baldly, but I need to justify myself. God, if you knew the remorse, the shame . . . I'm sorry. I am trying to get a grip on myself. Well, I . . . I must start somewhere.' He finished the last of his drink putting off, Wexford thought, the evil moment as long as he could. Then he said: 'I want you to know that it was quite correct what you said about my wife and me, being happy together, I mean, but with our marriage grown dull with the years. That was true. I accepted it. I thought it inevitable with people who had been married as long as we had, and who had no children. We never quarrelled. I think I should tell you now that if my wife had fallen in love with someone else I shouldn't have been angry. I shouldn't even have objected. I expect I would have been jealous, but I wouldn't have shown my jealousy by violence, God forbid!—or in any other way. I want to make that clear now.'

Wexford nodded noncommittally. The man's words were simple and frank, carrying, he thought, an unmistakable ring of truth.

'You said,' Quentin went on, 'that nobody involved in a murder case has any right to a private life. I'll have to tell you about my private life to make you understand why I did what I did.' He got up suddenly and walked swiftly to the bookshelves, pressing his hands flat against morocco and gilt bindings. Staring at the titles of the books but perhaps unseeing, he said, 'I used to go to her room once a fortnight, always on a Saturday night. She would push back the bedcovers and say, always the same, "This *is* nice, darling," and afterwards, when I left her to go back to my room, she'd say, "That was lovely, darling." She never called me by my name. Sometimes I think she forgot what it was.'

He stopped. Wexford wasn't the sort of policeman who says impatiently, 'Is all this really relevant, sir?' He said nothing, listening with a grave face.

'I was so bored,' Quentin said to the books. 'I was lonely. Sometimes I used to feel that I was married to a kind of beautiful animated statue, a doll that smiled and wore pretty clothes and even had a vocabulary of a certain limited kind.'

'And yet you were happy?' Wexford ventured quietly.

'Did I say that? Perhaps because everyone else said I was, I grew used to telling myself I must be.'

He moved away from the bookcase and began to pace the room. It seemed for a moment that he had changed the subject when he said, 'We used to keep servants, a proper staff, but Elizabeth gave them notice. Then we had a succession of *au pair* girls, two French and one German. I think Elizabeth made a point of choosing plain girls.' He swung round, faced Wexford and looked him straight in the eyes. 'Perhaps she thought Katje was plain. Fat and coarse was the way she once described her. I suppose—I suppose I was attracted to Katje from the start, but I never did anything about it. She was a young girl and I was—well, *in loco parentis*. I told myself I thought of her as a daughter. How we delude ourselves!' He turned away his face. 'It's almost impossible for me to find the words to tell you. I . . .'

'You slept with her?' Wexford said expressionlessly.

Quentin nodded.

'The night before last?'

'That wasn't the first time. Chief Inspector, in all the sixteen years we'd been married, I'd never been unfaithful to my wife. I'd had my opportunities. What man hasn't? I loved my wife. All those years I hoped for a sign of warmth, just one spontaneous sign that she recognised me as a human being. I never gave up hoping until Katje came. Then for the first time I saw a woman who was close to me, a woman living under my roof, behaving like a woman. Perhaps not as a woman should behave. She had boy friends all over the place and she used to tell me about them. Sometimes in the evenings Elizabeth would be out, walking in the grounds or gone early to bed, and Katje would come in from some date and she'd tell me about it, giggling and laughing, talking as if the best thing in the world was to take and give pleasure.

'One night, after one of these talks, I was lying in bed

waiting for Elizabeth to come in. I said I'd given up hope but that isn't true. I always hoped. I never remember feeling such a depth of loneliness as I felt that night. I thought I'd give everything I possessed, this house, the fortune I've amassed, if she would just come into my room and sit on the bed and talk to me.'

Again he covered his face. When he took away his hands Wexford expected to see tears on his cheeks, for he had spoken that last sentence on a sob, but he was quite calm, even relieved, it appeared, at having so nearly got it all off his chest.

'Presently I heard her come upstairs,' he said. 'I willed her to come in. I exercised all the power of my will. God knows how I stopped myself crying out to her. Her bedroom door closed and I heard her begin to run a bath. In that moment I forgot who I was, my age, my position, my duty to my wife. I put on my dressing gown and went upstairs. I knew what I was going to say to Katje, that I smelt gas and thought it was coming from her room. Of course I couldn't smell gas. All that was coming from her room was the faint sound of music from her radio.

'I knocked and she called to me to come in. She was sitting up in bed, reading a magazine. I didn't have to say anything about gas. It sounds incredible but I didn't speak a word. She smiled at me and put out her arms . . .'

Abruptly he stopped speaking. Like an old-fashioned novel, Wexford thought. If it were written down, asterisks would come at this point. Quentin Nightingale's asterisks were a sudden burning flush that threw into sharpness the whiteness of his hair and his moustache, ageing him. Fumbling for words and getting no help from the chief inspector, he said:

'There were—well, other times. Not many. There was

the night before last. I went up to Katje at about a
quarter past eleven. I didn't know whether Elizabeth had
come in. I wasn't thinking about Elizabeth. Katje and I—
well, I stayed with her all night. It was Palmer walking
about on the floor below that awakened me. I sensed
something was wrong, so I got up and dressed and found
him on the terrace.'

'A pity you didn't tell us all this before,' Wexford said
frowning.

'Put yourself in my place. Would you have?'

Wexford shrugged. 'That's beside the point.' He was at
a loss to account for his feelings. An alibi had been
destroyed and a more convincing one had replaced it.
Normally, when this occurred, he felt anger at the wasted
time, relief at progress made. His present unease wasn't
normal and briefly he questioned himself. Then he knew.
He was allowing himself something indefensible, personal involvement. What he felt for Quentin Nightingale
was envy. Stiffly he got up.

'This will have to be corroborated, Mr Nightingale,' he
said in a cold hard voice.

Pale again, Quentin said, 'I realised you would want to
ask Katje. It won't embarrass her. She's strange, unique.
She's . . . Oh, I'm wasting your time. I'm sorry.'

Wexford went upstairs. When he reached the first floor
he paused for a second outside the door of Quentin
Nightingale's bedroom and then, as he turned towards the
top flight and began to mount, he heard music coming
from above. It gave substance, near-reality to the un-
permitted dream his envy of Nightingale had evoked. A
soft, throaty voice was singing the number one song in
the pop charts, singing of love. A passionate longing,
bitter and savage, to recapture for one hour the youth he
had lost engulfed Wexford. And suddenly growing old

seemed the only tragedy of life, the pain beside which every other pain dwindled into insignificance. Mature, wise, usually philosophical, he wanted to cry aloud, 'It isn't fair!'

He came to the door and rapped on it sharply. The music should have stopped. Instead the voice welled and trembled on a vibrant note and she came to the door and let him in.

Her pink dress had white frills like a nightgown, and like a nightgown it was cut low to show milk-white half-moons and shoulders where even the bones looked soft. She smiled at him, her sea-blue eyes full of laughter. Quentin Nightingale had had all this, easily, without argument. So had the waiter at the Olive and Dove. So had how many others?

For the first time in his career he understood what impelled those men he questioned and brought to court, the men who forgot for a while chivalry and social taboo and sexual restraint, the rapists, the violators. But here there would perhaps be no need for violence, need only for a smile and an outstretched hand. *Ca me donne tant de plaisir et vous si peu de peine.* Oh, how much pleasure! He followed her into the room, and out of the dressing-table mirror their reflections marched towards them.

A young girl with her father. No, her grandfather. She was one of those people who make other people look unfinished and ill-made. In a bitter flash of illumination, Wexford saw himself as a battered bundle of old clothes. Not even middle-aged. Elderly, a grandfather.

'Please sit down, Miss Doorn,' he said, surprised that his voice was steady and sane. 'And would you turn that radio off?'

She complied, still smiling.

He felt just the same about her. The longing—perhaps

97

only a longing for rejuvenation?—was still there, but as he had turned away from the mirror he had experienced that sensation which divides the sane man from the mad. Between fantasy and reality a great gulf is fixed. And that which seems possible, reasonable, felicitous, when conjured in the mind, dissolves like smoke in a fresh wind when its object is present in words and solid flesh. He had seen her for a brief moment as a lovely thing, but a thing only, without the power of discrimination, without rights, without intelligence. Now he saw her as a young girl who saw him as he was, an old man. Inwardly his whole body seemed to laugh harshly at itself.

'I have some questions to ask you,' he said. He wished the laughter would stop so that he could control himself and mould himself into the image he desired, something between God and a robot, tempered with avuncular geniality. 'About your relations with Mr Nightingale.' Pity they had to talk about sex. But if they hadn't, perhaps the fantasy would never have grown. 'What terms are you on with him?'

'Terms?'

'You know very well what I mean,' he growled at her.

She shrugged at that, threw out her hands. 'I work for him and I live here in his house.' She pulled at a strand of hair, considered it and then poked it into her mouth. 'He is very nice and kind. I like him much.'

'He's your lover, isn't he?'

She said cautiously, not embarrassed and not at all frightened, 'He has said this?'

'Yes.'

'Oh, poor Kventin! He does not want anyone to know *at all*, must be kept very secret thing. And now you have found it out.'

'I'm afraid I must ask you to tell me about it.'

Stubbornly she stuck out her lower lip and shook her head.

'Come now. He's told me himself. You wouldn't want him to go to prison, would you?'

She opened her mouth wide. 'This is true? In England you can go to prison because you are making love?'

'Of course not!' Wexford almost shouted. 'Now listen. Mr Nightingale will not go to prison if you tell me the truth. Just tell me everything that happened between you . . . No, no, not *everything*.' An incredulous smile had widened her eyes. 'Simply how it began and so on.'

'All right.' She giggled with pure pleasure. 'This is always nice, I think, to talk about love. I like to talk of this more than anything.' Wexford could feel his angry frown, artificially assumed, pushing all his features forward. 'It is four, five weeks ago. I am in my bed and there is a knock and it is Kventin. Perhaps he is going to say the radio is too loud or I put the car away wrong, but he is saying nothing because at once I know he is coming to make love. I can see this in his face. Always I can see it in faces.'

God Almighty! thought Wexford, his soul cringing.

'So I am thinking, Why not? I am thinking how he is kind with nice manners and thin straight body and I am forgetting he is older than my father in Holland. And also I know he is lonely man married to a frigid cold woman. So we are making love very soon and all is different, for when he is in my bed he is not old any more.'

She said this triumphantly, pointing to the bed. Her favourite subject had driven away her laughter and she spoke earnestly, with concentration. 'Much much better than my friend the waiter,' she said. 'For Kventin has much experience and is knowing exactly how . . .'

'Yes, yes, I can imagine,' Wexford cut in. He drew a

deep breath. 'Miss Doorn, please spare me the lecture on sexual technique. Let us have the facts. There were other occasions?'

'Please?'

Grinding his teeth, Wexford said, 'Mr Nightingale—er, made love to you at other times?'

'*Of course*. He is liking me as much as I am liking him. The next week and the next week and then the night before last.'

'Go on.'

'But I have told you. I go out with my friend and the unkind man will not let us go into the hotel. My friend want us to go in the car, but this I will not do. This is not nice. Kventin would not do this. I am coming back home and I am thinking perhaps Kventin come up and make love with me. And I am wishing and wishing when he knocks at the door and then I am happy. We are both very very happy.'

'How long did he stay with you?'

'All the night,' said Katje airily. 'I tell him that just before I come in I see Mrs Nightingale go into the wood and he is saying very very sadly, She does not want me, she has never wanted me. But I say, *I* want you, Kventin, and so he stay all the night. But he is going away very early in the morning because he is hearing the old gardener man walk about. So I lie in my bed alone, thinking perhaps I shall not see my friend the waiter any more, but go only with Kventin, and then I too am getting up to see why the old gardener man is in the house. There, now I have told it all!'

Wexford was silent for a moment. Then he said, 'At what time did you see Mrs Nightingale cross the road?'

'Two minutes after eleven,' said Katje promptly.

'And at what time did Mr Nightingale pay you this

nocturnal visit?' She looked at him, her blue eyes naive and enquiring. 'I mean, come to your room?'

'Fifteen minutes after eleven. I come in, I go straight to bed.'

'How can you be so sure of the time?'

'I am wearing my new watch and always I am looking at it.' She waved her left wrist at him. The watch had a dial two inches in diameter fastened to a wide strap of pink and purple patent leather. 'This my friend is giving me for my birthday and all the time I look at it.' She glanced up at him under long dark gold lashes. 'You are angry with me?'

'No, no, I'm not angry, Miss Doorn.'

'I am wishing that you will call me Katje, please.'

'All right, Katje,' said Wexford, far from displeased.

Suddenly correct and very Continental, she held out her hand to him. Her fingers were soft and warm. 'Because,' she said, 'you resemble my old uncle in Friesland who is sometimes kind and sometimes cross like you.' She wagged a forefinger at him.

God, he thought, still smarting from that last thrust, how pretty that mannerism is now and how dreadful it will be when she's forty. And will she still chew her hair? In such reflections a little comfort lies.

'Now,' she said, her head on one side, 'I think I will go down and dust Kventin's study.'

9

BURDEN listened with disdain and incredulity to Wexford's condensed and to some extent expurgated account of his two interviews. It aroused in him a cold angry disgust. Anyone who knew the chief inspector less well than he might imagine Wexford to be quite smitten by the charms—invisible to Burden—of that immoral Dutch girl.

'I cannot see,' he said, standing by the window in Wexford's office and disentangling a knot in the string of the venetian blind, 'why you suppose this story of theirs lets them out at all.' He straightened the string and wound it round its hooks in a figure of eight. Burden liked everything to be neat and shipshape even in someone else's domain. 'On the contrary, they could have been in it together. You've only got that girl's word that he—er, joined her at eleven-fifteen. It could have been later. Of course she'd back him up.'

'Oh? Why would she? Just what would she get out of being an accessory to the murder of her employer's wife?'

Burden stared at him. Really, the old man was almost simple at times.

'Get out of it? Marriage with Nightingale, of course.'

'Don't keep saying "of course". It's far from of course. And leave that blind alone. Sometimes I think you've got a compulsion complex, always tidying everything up. Listen to me, Mike. You've got to bring your ideas up to date a bit. You may be only thirty-six but you're so dead old-fashioned it isn't true. First of all I want you to know that I believe Nightingale. I believe his story because some instinct in me recognises the truth when I hear it. I don't believe he's capable of violence. If he thought his wife had a lover—if he cared, which is more to the point —he'd divorce her. Secondly, Katje Doorn isn't a kind of Lady Macbeth. She's a very contemporary young woman who is enjoying life enormously and not the least of what she enjoys is plenty of anxiety-free sex.'

Burden went pink at that and blinked his eyes. He tried to put on a sophisticated expression and failed.

'What reason have we to suppose she wants to marry Nightingale?' Wexford went on. 'He's an old man to her,' he said urbanely. 'She said as much. And for all her immorality, as you'd put it, she's a nice normal girl who'd recoil in horror from the thought of taking into her bed a man fresh from murdering his wife. Mike, we've got to change our whole pattern of thinking in these domestic murder cases. Times have changed. Young women don't look on marriage as the be-all and end-all of existence any more. Girls like Katje won't help kill a man's wife just so that he can make honest women of them. They don't think they're *dishonest* women just because they're not virgins. And as for Katje wanting him for his money, I don't think she's given much thought to money yet. That may come later. At present she's out for a good time without any worry.'

'I sometimes wonder,' said Burden like an old man, 'what the world is coming to.'

'Let the world look after itself. We'll concentrate on our own small corner of it. We made a pattern, Mike, and now we've destroyed it. What next? There are two lines to pursue, it seems to me. Who was Mrs Nightingale's lover? Who had access to that torch?'

'You've had a lab report on it?'

Wexford nodded. 'There were traces of blood in the threads of the base screw and the lamp screw, and under the switch. The blood was of the same group as Mrs Nightingale's and it's a rare group, AB Negative. There's no doubt the torch was the weapon.'

'Well, who did have access to it? Who could have replaced it this morning?'

Wexford counted them off on his fingers. 'Nightingale, Katje, Mrs Cantrip, Will Palmer, Sean Lovell, Georgina Villiers—oh, and Lionel Marriott. Quite a list. We might also include Villiers, as Georgina could have replaced it for him. Now what about Sean? He's confessed to an admiration for Mrs Nightingale. He's young and hot-headed, therefore jealous. It may not have been he she went to meet but he could have seen her with that person. His alibi is hopeless. He had access to the torch; his garden gives directly on to the forest.'

'She was old enough to be his mother,' said Burden.

Wexford laughed, a raucous bray. 'My God, Mike, you don't know what life's about, do you? It's because he was twenty and she forty that he *would* have an affair with her. Like . . .' He paused, then went on with apparent detachment, 'Like middle-aged men and young girls. It happens all the time. Didn't you ever fancy any of your mother's friends?'

'Certainly not!' said Burden, outraged. 'My mother's friends were like aunts to me. I called them all auntie. Still do, come to that. What's so funny?'

'You,' said Wexford, 'and if I didn't laugh I'd go round the twist.'

Burden was used to this but still he was very offended.

seemed unfair to him, a sad sign of the times, that a
an should be laughed at because he had high principles
d a decent concept of what life should be. He gave a
in dry cough and said:

'I shall go and have another talk with your favourite
spect, young Lovell.'

'You do that.' Wexford looked at his watch. 'I have a
te at four.' He grinned. 'A date with someone who is
ing to enlighten me further as to certain past histories.'

Wexford parked a hundred yards up the road from the
hool gates, well behind the cars of parents waiting for
even-year-olds. A crocodile of cricketers in green-stained
hite came across from the playing fields as the clock on
e school tower struck four. If they were punctual in
thing else, King's pupils were punctual in getting out of
hool. As the last chime died away, they poured through
e gates, laughing, shoving each other, paying no atten-
n to the kerb drill with which Wexford had used to
lieve they were thoroughly indoctrinated by the road
fety officer. Only the supercilious sixth-formers walked
dately, lighting cigarettes when they reached the
adow of the overhanging trees.

Denys Villiers came out in his dark blue Anglia. He
unded his horn repetitively to clear boys out of the road,
en, putting his head out of the window, shouted some-
ing Wexford couldn't catch. The tone of his voice was
ough. Wexford had the notion that if the man had had
whip he would have used it. He turned his head and
w Marriott trotting out of the main gate. When the
tle man had passed the car he wound down the window
d hissed:

' "A frightful fiend doth close behind you tread!" '
Marriott jumped, collected himself and smiled.

105

'A very overrated poem, I've always thought,' he said

'I daresay. I didn't come here to discuss poetry. You were going to give me the slip, weren't you?'

Marriott came round the bonnet and got into the car

'I must admit I was. I thought you'd give me a lecture for going up to the Manor this morning. Now please don't there's a dear. I've had a most exhausting afternoo introducing *Paradise Lost* to the Lower Fifth and I reall can't stand any more.'

' "The mind," ' quoted Wexford, ' "is in its own plac and in itself can make a heaven of hell, a hell of heaven." '

'Yes, very clever. I'm different. Mine makes a hell o hell. Do let's rush, ducky, and get ourselves huge drink I suppose you'll want me to go on with the next insta ment on the way.'

'I can't wait,' said Wexford, starting the car an moving out into the stream.

'Where had I got to?'

'Villiers' first wife.'

'June,' said Marriott. 'She didn't like me. Oh dear, no She said I'd be more use teaching in a Borstal institution The first time she went to the Manor d'you know wha she said to Quentin? "I call it scandalous," she said, "tw people living by themselves in this barrack. It ought to b converted into a mental hospital." Poor Quen didn't lik that at all. His beloved house! But that was little June a over. She had a sociology degree and she'd been some kin of probation officer.

'She and Denys had a dreadful flat over the pet foo shop in Queen Street. You know the place I mean. I onl went there once and that was enough. The stink putrefying horseflesh, my dear, and June's funny frien all over the place. Crowds of them there every evenin all very earnest and wanting to put the world right. Ba ing the Bomb was the thing in those days, you know, nd June used to hold meetings about it in their flat, that nd famine relief before famine relief was even fashion-ble. She was the original demonstrator, was June. When-ver there's a rumpus in Grosvenor Square I look very losely at the pictures, I can tell you, because I'm positive m going to see her face there one of these days.'

'She's not dead, then?' Wexford said as they emerged nto the High Street.

'Good God, no. Denys divorced her or she divorced him. forget which. Heaven knows why they got married in e first place. They had nothing in common. She didn't ke Quen and Elizabeth and she took a very dim view of enys going up to the Manor so much. Associating with :actionary elements, she called it.'

'If he didn't care for his sister why did he go so much?'

'Well, you see, he and Quen got on together like a ouse on fire from the word go,' said Marriott as Wexford ulled into the centre of the road to take the right-hand rn. 'Quen was thrilled to bits finding he'd got an up-nd-coming writer for a brother-in-law and I suppose he w himself in the light of Denys's patron.' The car oved slowly down the alley and Wexford pulled up in ont of the white flower-decked house. 'Anyway, Denys ust have complained to him about how impossible it as to work in his home atmosphere, and Quen offered im the Old House to write in. Don't let's sit out here, eg, I'm dying of thirst.'

The rooms where the party had been held still smelt rongly of cigar smoke. Someone had tidied up and ashed all the dishes. Hypatia, probably, Wexford ought, as Marriott flung open all the windows.

'Now then, Reg, the cocktail hour, as they say. A little

early perhaps, but everything's early in the country, don'
you find? What's it to be? Whisky? Gin?'

'I'd rather have a cup of tea,' said Wexford.

'Would you? How odd. All right, I'll put the kettle on
I must say, Hypatia has left everything very nice. I mus
remember to say a word when next I see her.'

Wexford followed him into the kitchen. 'She doesn'
live here, then?'

'Oh, no. I shouldn't care for that at all.' Marriot
wrinkled his nose distastefully. 'Once have them per
manently in and you can't call your soul your own.' H
gave Wexford a sidelong very sly look. 'Besides, there'
safety in numbers.'

Wexford laughed. 'Quite a devil with the ladies, aren'
you, Lionel?'

'I have my successes,' said Marriott modestly. He pu
three spoonfuls of Earl Grey into the teapot and poure
the boiling water on daintily. 'Shall I go on with th
story?'

'Please.'

'Well, as I said, June didn't at all care for Denys work
ing at the Manor. He was up there most evenings natter
ing with Quen, you see, and every day in the holidays t
work. She thought he ought to be out with her, wavin
banners and writing things on walls. So finally she walke
out on him.'

'Leaving him to his *ménage à trois*?'

'What a funny way of putting it. Still, no doubt, ther
was a triangular element there, but not an isoscele
triangle. Poor Elizabeth was definitely the unequal angl
It always used to fascinate me when I went up there t
see Denys and Quen utterly immersed in each othe
books, books, books, my dear, and a positively ringin
exchange of Wordsworth quotes, the two of them groa

ng that they had thoughts which do often lie too deep
or tears. And all the time poor Elizabeth sat there read-
ng *Vogue* and not a word to say for herself.'

'I daresay you found something to chat to her about,'
aid Wexford, drinking his tea. 'I never met anyone who
new so much about—what shall I say?—current trivia?'

'Really, Reg, you *are* unkind. I'll have you know,
lizabeth wasn't at all an empty-headed woman. Just as
ntelligent as Denys in her way.'

'That's not what he says, but let it pass.'

'Why are we sitting out here, anyway? I never could
bide kitchens and I'm pining for my gin. Good, the cigar
moke's cleared.'

Marriott fetched his drink and pulled two chairs up to
ne open french windows. His small walled garden was
ull of butterflies, drinking from the buddleia flowers and
nning themselves with spread wings on the stones.
Vexford sat where he could feel the warmth of the
recious September sun that would soon be gone. It made
im feel lazy and he told himself sternly to keep his mind
lert.

'So Villiers spent a good deal of his time at the Manor,
id he?' he said.

'Believe me, you couldn't set foot in the place without
nding him there. And as if that wasn't enough to make
im and Quen heartily sick of each other, he used to go
way on holiday with them too.'

'That must have been hard on Mrs Nightingale, especi-
lly as they excluded her from their conversations. Just
hat were her interests, Lionel?'

Marriott bit his lip and seemed to cogitate. 'Let me see,'
e said with the air of someone dredging in the depths.
Vell, she took an active part in county life, you know,
rganising things and sitting on committees. And she

spent hours every day making herself look lovely. She did
the flowers and a bit of gardening . . .'

'Is that so?' Wexford interrupted. 'In the hothouse
maybe with young Sean Lovell?'

'What can you mean, dear old boy?'

'As one of Wordsworth's contemporaries put it:

' "What men call gallantry and gods adultery,
    Is much more common where the climate's sultry."

Marriott smiled, opening his eyes wide. 'So that's the
way the wind's blowing, is it?'

'Well, she wasn't having secret meetings in the forest
with old Sir George Larkin-Smith, was she? Or the rector
of Myfleet or Will Palmer? Unless it was you, Lionel.'

'I wondered when you were going to ask me that.'
Marriott stretched languorously in the sunshine and
laughed. 'But no, it wasn't. And if you're serious about
this, Reg, Hypatia will tell you where I was. Mind you
I'm not saying I didn't wish I'd had the opportunity . . .'

'Maybe you even tried your chances?'

'Maybe I did.'

This time it was Wexford's turn to laugh. 'So we come
back to Sean Lovell, don't we?'

'She was fond of Sean,' said Marriott. 'I met her once
coming out of the record shop here in the High Street.
She'd been buying the number one pop single in the charts.
"I must keep up with my little song-bird," she said.
"Really, he's the only true Nightingale in Myfleet." Quite
witty, I thought. Elizabeth was no fool.'

'An extraordinary remark to make,' said Wexford.

'Oh, I don't know. You read too much into things, my
dear. All you policemen are terribly salacious. Sean used
to stand under Elizabeth's windows and serenade her.

suppose she was flattered and it made her feel young. It was a case of heroine worship on one side and a sort of flattered acceptance on the other.'

'Let's get back to Villiers,' said Wexford. 'But first how about another cup of tea for a poor old salacious policeman?'

Myfleet was a pretty village even on a winter's day. Now, bathed in mellow sunshine, it lay in its hollow beneath the forest like a sleeping beauty. This afternoon it seemed unpeopled; only the flowers in cottage gardens stood out in the open enjoying the sun.

Burden drove to the Kingsmarkham end of the village and decided to walk the rest of the way. It was a day made for strolling, for appreciating the scent of ripening fruit and admiring the great multi-petalled dahlias, raised for a flower show or a harvest festival.

But he had been wrong in thinking the village totally deserted. Now, as he approached the Manor, he noticed Mrs Lovell leaning over the gate of her disreputable cottage, talking to a swarthy man in a cap who carried two dead and bleeding rabbits over his arm. The shifty looks he was giving the Manor—though probably the natural accompaniment to his conversation, concerned as it must be with the only topic currently of interest in Myfleet—gave him the air of a poacher. Mrs Lovell encouraged him with peals of uninhibited ringing laughter.

He found Sean in the Old House, unloading apples from a basket on to one of the racks. They were pale red and gold, Beauty of Bath, their skins striped and shiny like old silk. The boy was whistling but he stopped abruptly when Burden came in.

'Come here often, do you?' Burden asked softly. 'Is this where you used to meet Mrs Nightingale?'

'*Me?*' He gave Burden a sullen glare, sat down on a stack of silver-birch logs and began to roll a cigarette. 'It'd be a help,' he said, 'if I knew what you was getting at. No, I don't come here often. Fact is I never set foot in here since April.' He cocked a thumb at the tunnel staircase. 'On account of *him* being up there.' Scowling, he lit his cigarette. 'Me and old Palmer, we've got strict orders not to come in here disturbing him, see?'

'You go into the garden room, though, don't you? You go to sweep it out. Ever borrowed a torch, Lovell, to light your way when you went to Mrs Nightingale in the forest?'

'*Me?*' Sean said again. 'Are you off your nut?' His cigarette had gone out. He re-lit it, blinking when the flame caught the ragged paper and flared. Perhaps it provided a flash of mental as well as physical illumination, for he said, 'You trying to make out I was carrying on with Mrs Nightingale? You *are* a nut and a dirty-minded nut at that.'

'All right, that'll do,' said Burden, mortally offended. The supreme injustice of the accusation wounded him more than the insolence. 'Come now,' he said, keeping his temper, 'you were on very friendly terms with her.'

'Look,' said Sean, 'if you must know, she was interested in helping me with my career.'

'Helping you do the *gardening*?'

The boy's face flushed deeply. Unknowingly, Burden had returned thrust for thrust. 'Gardening's not my career,' Sean said bitterly. 'That's just a stop-gap, just to fill in time till I get on with my real work.'

'And what might that be?'

'Music,' said Sean. 'The Scene. Up there in London.' Again he cocked a thumb, this time northwards. His face had grown rapt and, like Dick Whittington, he seemed to

see a vision, a city paved with gold. 'I've got to get there.'
His voice shook. 'I know it all, see, like it was recorded
in my head. I could tell you the way all the charts were,
right back for years. I could pass exams.' He clenched his
hands and there shone in his eyes the fanaticism of the
religious mystic. 'There's not one of them D.J.s knows
half of what I do.' Suddenly he shouted at Burden, 'Take
that grin off your face! You're just ignorant like the rest
of them, like my old lady with her men and her booze.
Mrs Nightingale was the only one as understood and she's
dead.' He drew a dirty sleeve across his eyes, the artist
manqué that the world persists in treating as an artisan.

Gentler this time, Burden said, 'What was Mrs Nightingale going to do for you?'

'There was this bloke in London she knew,' Sean said,
muttering now. 'He was with the B.B.C. and she promised
faithful she'd mention my name. Maybe for singing,
maybe for a D.J. In a small way for a start.' he added
humbly. 'You got to start in a small way.' He sighed. 'I
don't know what'll happen to me now.'

'Best stick to your gardening, grow up a bit and get rid
of some of these fancy ideas,' Burden said. Sean's glance
of pure hatred riled him. 'Let's forget your ambitions for
a moment, shall we? Why did you tell the chief inspector
you were watching a television programme when that
programme wasn't even shown?'

Sean looked peevish rather than frightened at being
caught out in his lie. 'I had been watching the telly,' he
said, 'but I got fed up. My old lady had got her bloke in
for the evening, that Alf Tawney. Grinning at me, they
was, and mocking me on account of me watching Pop
Panel.' Sean clenched his fingers over an apple until his
knuckles whitened. 'One fellow after another my mum's
had ever since I was a kid and all they've ever wanted is

to get me out of the way. I tell you, when I was about ten I saw my mum with one of them men of hers, kissing and pawing each other and I picked up the carving knife and went for her. I'd have killed her, I would, only the bloke got the knife away and hit me. I'd have killed her,' he said fiercely, and then something he saw in Burden's eyes silenced him. Awkwardly he said, 'I don't care any more, not about her, only I get—I get fed up.' His fingers relaxed and he dropped the apple into the rack. Burden saw that his nails had pierced the rosy skin, leaving deep juicy wounds.

He said smoothly, 'It seems to me you let your emotions get the better of you.'

'I said I was ten, didn't I? I'm not like that now. I wouldn't lay a finger on her whatever she did.'

'I take it,' said Burden, as Sean wiped his sticky hand on his jeans, 'I take it you're referring to your mother?'

'Who else'd I be referring to?'

Burden shrugged lightly. 'So you got "fed up" with your mother and Alf Tawney. Where did you go?'

'Down to my shed,' said Sean. 'I sat there all alone, thinking.' He sighed heavily, got up and, turning his back on Burden, resumed his unloading of the apples. 'Just thinking and—and listening.' The bright fruit, bruised by his hands, rolled into the rack. Very softly he began whistling again. His face had coloured as vivid a red as the apples. Getting up to leave, Burden wondered why.

'Denys always went on holiday with them,' said Marriott. 'With both of them, I mean. But two years ago he had to go with Elizabeth alone. Quen caught the measles, poor thing. So humiliating. Elizabeth told me she absolutely dreaded being stuck with Denys in Dubrovnik, but Quen said he'd never forgive them if they stayed at home on his account, so they had to put up with it.

'Well, they must have rowed the whole time because they both looked rotten when they got back and there was a distinct coldness between Denys and Quen all the following winter and Denys stopped going up to the Manor. Then, one day, in the June of the summer before last, I was up at the Manor when in walked Denys. "You are a stranger," Quen said, but I could tell he was over-joyed. "I only came," said Denys, "to tell you I can't go to Rome with you next month. I've promised the Head I'll be one of the escorts to the school party."

' "You?" I almost screamed. "You must be out of your mind." I mean, it's a joke at school, the lengths the staff go to get out of it. "You'd pass up lovely Rome," I said, "for the lousy old Costa Brava?" "I'm going," he said, "it's all fixed." You should have seen poor Quen's face. He did his best to work on Denys but it was no use. He was adamant.'

'What about this year, Lionel?'

'He was married by then, wasn't he? He met Georgina on the Costa Brava, but I'll come to that later. No, this year they went off to Bermuda by themselves, and I think that secretly they were only too glad to have got rid of old misery face. Elizabeth said as much to me when I went up there to witness her will and . . .'

'Her what?' said Wexford slowly. 'Did you say her will?'

10

'WHY didn't I tell you that my wife had made a will? Frankly, Chief Inspector, because I'd forgotten all about it.' Quentin Nightingale had seemed bewildered at first, but now he smiled a slightly derisory smile as if at someone making a mountain out of a molehill. He had negotiated his own mountain and descended it with only a few bruises. Why bother him now with trivialities? 'I don't for a moment suppose it's legal. It was just a piece of nonsense my wife took into her head, you know.'

'No, I don't know,' said Wexford, refusing the offer of a leather chair and standing instead against the tall book-case. 'I imagine that people in your position have their solicitors draw up their wills for them. Who is your solicitor, Mr Nightingale?'

'But no solicitor was involved. I told you it was just a piece of nonsense. Really, I can't think how you came to hear of it.' He paused expectantly, but when it became clear to him that Wexford didn't intend to enlighten him, he said, with an edge of impatience to his voice, 'I'd better tell you about it.'

'I wish you would,' said Wexford, leaning his head against the hard smooth bindings of Motley's *Rise of the Dutch Republic.*

'Well, it was last summer. My wife and I had decided on Bermuda for our holiday and naturally we intended to fly. Although my wife had flown before—when we went to America seven years ago—she didn't like flying and we usually went on holiday by sea and car.'

'She was afraid to fly?'

'Oh, come. "Afraid" is putting it too strongly.'

'If she made a will,' Wexford retorted, 'I suppose it was because she thought she might die. "Afraid" isn't too strong a word to use about the anticipation of death.'

'You're looking at it much too dramatically,' Quentin said with exasperation. 'She was a little anxious but she was quite prepared to joke about it. This will was a sort of joke. I told you I never took it seriously.'

He stopped talking and listened for a second. By straining his ears Wexford too could just hear the sound of Katje's radio from far above them. Then Quentin's eyes met his and the other man flushed slightly. He went on in quick impatient tones. 'One day she said she was making a will and I saw her scribbling something on a sheet of paper. I'm afraid I didn't even look at it. I took it for one of those romantic fads very feminine women go in for. I remember my mother,' he said, going off at a tangent, 'when my youngest sister was born, going and having her photograph taken to be a last memento for my father in case she died in childbirth, and writing farewell letters for all her other children. But of course she didn't die any more than Elizabeth . . .'

'But your wife did die, Mr Nightingale,' Wexford said quietly.

Quentin looked down and clasped his hands together.

'Yes . . . About this will, I took it for nonsense, as I've said. I doubt if it was even witnessed.'

'One person witnessed it, at any rate,' said Wexford. 'Lionel Marriott.'

Quentin raised his eyes and there was genuine surprise in them.

117

'Mr Nightingale, I can't just let this go by. What became of this piece of paper your wife was "scribbling" on?'

'She gave it to me and asked me to put it in my safe.'

'And did you?'

'Well, yes, I did. Elizabeth insisted on my doing so in her presence. Oh, it was very silly but I didn't want to distress her.'

'Is it still there?'

'I suppose so,' Quentin said wonderingly. 'I told you, I forgot all about it and I imagine Elizabeth did too when we got back safe and sound.'

Wexford said heavily, 'I'll trouble you to open that safe now, sir, if you please.'

Eyeing Wexford as if he thought he was dealing with a lunatic who needed to be humoured, Quentin lifted down from the study wall a small Stubbs oil of a phaeton and pair. Behind it, set into the wall, was a steel door. Murmuring the combination under his breath, Quentin opened it to reveal a space about the size of a large biscuit tin. The safe contained a neat stack of papers which Wexford supposed to be share certificates and personal documents, and several leather jewel boxes. Quentin took out a handful of papers. He leafed through them and then, his expression still amused and derisive, held out to Wexford a long brown envelope.

'It's in there,' he said.

'May I?' Wexford's tone left no room for refusal. He slit open the envelope and drew out a sheet of expensive blue writing paper headed with the Manor address. The paper was covered with a bold, rather masculine handwriting. Wexford turned it over, glanced at the foot of the reverse side and said in his strong official voice, 'This is a perfectly legal will, sir, none the less valid and binding because it was not made on a will form or in the presence of a lawyer.'

'Good heavens!' said Quentin. He sat down, leaving the safe door open.

'It is witnessed by—let me see—Myrtle Annie Cantrip and Lionel Hepburn Marriott and correctly signed by your wife. You'd find yourself up against a great deal of trouble if you tried to contest it.'

'But I don't want to contest it.'

'I think you'd better read it before you commit yourself, Mr Nightingale.'

'What does it say?' Quentin's face was now utterly bewildered, the smile wiped away. 'Will you read it me, Mr Wexford?'

'Very well.' At last Wexford sat down. He cleared his throat and read in the same expressionless voice:

'"*This is the last will and testament of me, Elizabeth Frances Nightingale, born Villiers, being of sound mind. This is my last will and revokes all other wills made by me.*"' Here Mrs Nightingale's knowledge of legal language had apparently dried up, for she continued in a more natural manner, interspersed, however, with occasional officialese. '"*I leave all my money, including the money my husband invested for me, to Sean Arthur Lovell, of 2 Church Cottages, Myfleet, in the county of Sussex, in the hope that he will use it in the furtherance of his ambition. . . .*"'

'Good heavens!' Quentin said again. 'Good heavens!'

'". . . *and all the personal jewellery I possess to my sister-in-law, Georgina Villiers, of 55 Kingsmarkham Road, Clusterwell . . .*"' Here Wexford paused and raised his eyebrows. '". . . *so that she may indulge her love of adornment, although as a virtuous woman her price is above rubies." '*

'Elizabeth wrote that?' Quentin asked in a hollow voice.

'Yes, sir.'

They were both surprised, Wexford thought, but probably for different reasons. For his part he was astonished that the woman whom her brother had described as frivolous and empty-headed should have had the wit to compose it and the knowledge to give it that malevolent bite. Quentin's astonishment stemmed perhaps from the malevolence alone. He had gone pale.

'Is that all?' he asked.

'That's all. How much money did your wife leave, sir?'

'Oh, nothing to speak of.' Quentin forced a laugh. 'She was overdrawn, as a matter of fact, on her private account. There's about three hundred pounds that I invested for her years ago.'

'Mmhm. I'm sure you won't grudge that to young Lovell. Is something troubling you, sir?'

'No, well, I . . .'

'Mrs Villiers,' said Wexford thoughtfully, 'is a lady who seems fond of jewellery, as your wife—er, pointed out. Let us hope there are a few nice pieces for her.'

'A few nice pieces!' Quentin suddenly sprang to his feet. 'My wife's jewellery is in those boxes.' He plunged his hands into the safe. 'At a rough estimate,' he said, 'I'd value it at thirty thousand pounds.'

Wexford had seen too many precious stones to be dazzled by this small but brilliant collection. He was, in any case, not given to gasping, and his face was calm with a hint of taciturnity as he watched Quentin open the three boxes.

One was of white leather, one of green and the third of teak inlaid with onyx. Quentin had placed them on his writing desk and lifted the lids to disclose more boxes, tiny caskets for rings and ear-rings, longer cases for bracelets and necklaces.

Quentin took out one of the rings, a diamond half-hoop, set in platinum, and held it to the light.

'It was her engagement ring,' he said. 'She wore it sometimes, when,' he said, his voice growing hoarse, 'I particularly asked her to.' He looked at Wexford. 'Perhaps I could buy it from Georgina.'

'Your wife was fond of her?'

'I don't know,' Quentin said hopelessly, pushing the ring back into its velvet bed. 'I never thought much about it. She must have been . . . And yet she can't have been, can she? You couldn't be fond of someone and leave that cruel message for them. I don't understand it.'

'We know Mrs Nightingale had a strong dislike for her brother. Perhaps that dislike extended itself to his wife.'

Quentin closed the ring box. 'The idea seems to have got about,' he said carefully, 'that my wife and her brother were at daggers drawn.'

Wexford raised his eyebrows. 'It isn't true?'

'It seems strange for me, her husband, to say this, but really I don't know. Denys never found fault with her to me and as for Elizabeth . . . Well, she never tried to stop him coming to the house, although it's true she did sometimes say rather spiteful things to me about him when we were alone. And yet, you know, I used to see her look—well, almost compassionately at him when we were all three together. I never saw signs of any real hatred.'

'Perhaps you're not a man who probes much into other people's motives and emotions.'

'I can't be, can I?' Quentin said sadly. 'Otherwise I'd

have seen that Elizabeth didn't enjoy Georgina's company and I'd have . . . I'd have realised she was going secretly into the forest at night. No, I suppose Elizabeth and Denys did have a genuine dislike of each other and I hadn't the perception to see it. Or I didn't want to.' He spoke quietly now and with slight embarrassment. 'When you love people you want them to love each other and you convince yourself they do. I hate the idea of malicious stories going round that there was some sort of feud.'

There was a short silence and then Wexford said, 'Back to this will, sir. You evidently didn't know of your wife's friendship with Sean Lovell?'

'I knew she took a maternal interest in him. We have no children of our own. She asked me to get a friend of mine at the B.B.C. to hear him sing and I wasn't too keen but I will now. It's the least thing—and the last thing—I can do for her.'

'Forgive me—you never suspected the interest might be more than maternal?'

Quentin screwed up his face in distaste, shaking his head violently. 'Oh God,' he said, 'there can't have been but if there was . . . I've no right to sit in judgment, not while I and Katje . . . Mr Wexford, I don't understand these undercurrents. I don't understand any of it.'

'Nor do I,' said Wexford grimly.

Meanwhile Burden was making discoveries of his own.

Emerging from the Old House and from the gate to the courtyard which surrounded it, he encountered Mrs Cantrip coming from the kitchen garden with a bunch of parsley in her hand.

'Oh, you startled me, sir,' she said. 'You walk so soft. Would you like a cup of tea?'

'Getting a bit late for that, isn't it?' said Burden look-
g at his watch and seeing that it was half past five.
'hen do you knock off, anyway?'
'Supposed to be at four and that's a fact, but we're all
sixes and sevens these days, don't know where we are.
me on, sir, do. It'll do you good and there's Will wait-
g to have a word with you.'
'What does he want me for?' Burden walked towards
e house with her.
'He wouldn't say, sir. Something about a scarf, I
:kon.'
In the kitchen Will Palmer sat at the table next to the
in Burden had observed earlier talking over her gate to
s Lovell. They were drinking tea from cups of dark
ized earthenware. The other man's presence in the
chen was explained by the two rabbits, four wood
;eons and a basket of eggs that filled a checkered
inter top.
As soon as he saw Burden, Palmer got to his feet.
Got something to show you, governor.'
'Well?' Burden took his teacup from Mrs Cantrip,
noving it as far as possible from the dead game.
'This is it.' With an air of triumph, Palmer produced
m under the table a wet polythene bag, its neck
tened with garden twine. Burden undid the string and
lled out a piece of material. It was dampish but not
t and it was still plainly recognisable as a silk scarf.
e design on it was *art nouveau*, a stylised exquisite
ttern of gold leaves on a primrose ground. Across the
itre of the scarf was a long brown stain. Burden
wned.
Where did you find this?'
In a hole in the oak way down Cleever's Vale.'
And where might Cleever's Vale be?'

Palmer's face registered a stunned astonishment. It wa evidently inconceivable to him that anyone, especially policeman, should be ignorant of something that t Myfleet was as much a part of the scene as the fores itself.

Mrs Cantrip said impatiently, 'It's part of the estate, si part of the park, the bit you come to first when you' coming this way from Kingsmarkham.'

'I was by way of clearing that old fungus from the oak Palmer said, recovering from his astonishment. 'Then come on this hole, see? Likely an owl made it . . .'

'Squirrel,' said the other man laconically, wiping h mouth. His face was very dark with a good day's grow of beard.

'Or a squirrel, as I was going to say, Alf,' said Palme ruffled. 'An owl or a squirrel, it being over-large for woodpecker.'

'Spare me the natural history.'

'All right, governor, no need to get sarky.' Palme expression gained a new importance as the door to t garden opened and Sean came in to take his place at t table. 'This hole would be about six feet up, I reckor Palmer continued. 'Level with the top of my head, it wa

'Rot,' said the swarthy man.

Palmer glared at him, but, apparently deciding that t interjection referred to the cause of the hole rather th to the nonsensical content of his remarks, went on, 'Th old fungus were all round the hole. What we call th Oyster Mushroom, sir, on account of his cap looks like oyster, see? The Poor Man's Oyster we calls him in the parts and mighty good fried he is, I can tell you.'

'Stewed.'

'Or stewed, Alf,' said Palmer more graciously. 'To cu

long story short, I stuck me hand in this hole and that's what I found, what's in that bag.'

'In the bag? Or did you put it in?'

'It wasn't in no bag, governor. Just rolled up and stuffed down the hole.'

'Have you ever seen it before?'

'Of course he has,' said Mrs Cantrip. 'It belonged to poor Mrs Nightingale. She used to wear it for a headscarf like when she went out walking.' She bent over the scarf and recoiled sharply. 'Would that be her blood, sir?'

'I'm afraid so.'

Sean Lovell jerked to his feet.

'Going to be sick!' he shouted. Moving faster than Burden would have believed possible in a woman of her age, Mrs Cantrip flung open the garden door.

'Not in my kitchen, you're not!'

With the unmoved scowl of the English rustic, the old gardener and the purveyor of game watched him stagger out, then listened with a quickened though still apathetic interest to the sounds of retching. Alf, hitherto monosyllabic, made what was for him a long speech.

'Old stomach complaint,' he said. 'No guts.' He laughed. 'Wants to be a bleeding pop singer. Mental, I reckon he'

Mrs Cantrip took his cup and saucer and put them in the dishwasher. When the man made no move to go, she said briskly, 'I'll say good night, then, Alf. And we don't want no more eggs till Monday.'

Leaving the Manor by the front and back doors respectively, Wexford and Burden encountered each other in the village street. There they exchanged news and were about to embark on one of their acrimonious but valuable

discussions when Mrs Cantrip, puffed with runnin
caught them up.

'Oh, sir,' she said to Burden, 'I *am* glad I caught you.
want to apologise, like, for the way those two went o
old Will and that Alf. Will's that talkative and as for A
Tawney . . . He's not got the manners he was born wit
Would I be in your way if I was to walk along with y
a bit?'

'Not at all, Mrs Cantrip,' said Wexford graciously. I
stopped by the official car and told Bryant to drive it ba
to the station. 'Who's Alf Tawney?'

'Just a fellow we get our veg and chickens and su
from, sir. He lives in a caravan on his ground at Cluste
well.' Mrs Cantrip's face closed into a kind of prudi
blankness, just as Burden's own sometimes did when
subject he would have described as 'suggestive' was abo
to be discussed. 'You wouldn't be interested in Alf,' s
said primly.

'I don't know,' said Wexford. 'Anyone associated wi
Mrs Nightingale interests us, even if he only supplied h
with vegetables.'

'Mrs Nightingale never associated with him, sir,' sa
Mrs Cantrip, shocked. 'If she'd ever heard of him it w
only through that Sean.' She sighed, as if coming to a pai
ful decision. 'Well, you may as well know, seeing as i
common gossip and the scandal of the village. Alf's carr
ing on with Sean's mother.'

'Dear me,' said Wexford. 'That's bad.'

'There's some as don't blame Alf, him being a wid
man since his boy was twelve and what with no one
cook his meals and see to his things. It's her I blame. F
like the Bible says, sir, woman is a temptation to m
and no two ways about it.'

'True,' said Wexford with feeling.

'Mind you, I don't care for that Sean myself, but there's
ne as 'd deny Mrs Lovell's neglected him shameful. You
ght say he's never had no proper mother.'

'And Mrs Nightingale never had a son.'

Mrs Cantrip turned her face up to him. Once more, as
ey approached ground she had decided must be for-
lden, she looked guarded and resentful. 'That Sean
ouldn't have dared think of Madam in that way,' she
d. 'There *are* limits. Besides, Mrs Nightingale—well,
e looked so young and lovely, sir. She didn't like people
owing her age. It went to my heart sometimes the way
e wanted Sean and Catcher to feel she was the same age
 what they were. And when Sean said—it wasn't
pectful, sir, but he doesn't know no better—when he
d she wasn't square and once when he said she was
er to look at than any lady for miles round, she looked
pleased and happy.'

'He is a very handsome young man,' said Wexford.

I can't see it myself, sir, but tastes differ. Well, here's
ere I live, so I'll say good night. And I hope you've
en no offence at the way them two went on, sir.'

They watched her go into the freshly painted white
tage whose patchwork-quilt garden was one of those
rden had earlier admired. She gathered into her arms a
hiony yellow cat which had strolled out to meet her,
d closed the front door.

The poor neglected boy,' said Wexford thoughtfully,
herits three hundred pounds under Mrs Nightingale's
l. I wonder if he knows and if he thought it worth
ling for? But we'll leave that for the moment and call
the principal beneficiary.'

Sir?' Burden looked at him enquiringly.

I'll tell you in the car.' Wexford grinned broadly.

'How beautiful on the mountain are the feet of him wh
bringeth good tidings!'

How would she receive the news? Wexford wondere
With surprised gratification? Or with fear that the w
had been disclosed to official eyes? It might be that sh
was genuinely ignorant of its contents or even of i
existence.

He told her baldly that Mrs Nightingale's will was
her favour and watched her reactions. They were di
appointing. She shrugged her shoulders and said, 'That's
surprise. I had no idea.' As usual she wore the necklac
bracelets and ear-rings which were as indispensable to h
as stockings and lipstick might be to another woman, a
not even the faintest flash of concupiscence crossed h
face to show that she would be glad to replace them wi
real stones. Her expression was apathetic and indifferer
almost sleepy, as if she had recently passed through so
ordeal, so tumultuous that it had left her drained of
feeling.

'You didn't know she had made a will? Or you do
know what she's left you?'

'No to both,' said Georgina. She sat down on the arm
a chair. Her blouse was sleeveless and Wexford notic
the strong sinews of her shoulders and upper arms. On
once before had he seen such sinews on a woman's ar
and that woman had been a female wrestler.

'You inherit all Mrs Nightingale's jewellery,' he said.

'I see. When you said the will was in my favour
thought it must be something like that. Elizabeth had
any money of her own and she always got through h
allowance before the next was due. She was awfu
extravagant.'

'Mrs Villiers, this puts a rather different complexion

e circumstances of your sister-in-law's death.'

'Does it? I'm afraid I don't quite understand.'

'Let me explain then.' Wexford paused as the door
)ened and Denys Villiers came in, his recently published
)ok open in his hand.

'Oh, there you are, Denys,' his wife said, getting up. Her
)ice was still dull and toneless as she said, 'Fancy,
lizabeth made a will and left me all those rings and
ecklaces of hers.'

Villiers put his thumb between the pages of his book to
ark the place and looked with dry amusement into the
ern faces of the two policemen. Then, without warning,
e burst into a roar of hysterical laughter.

11

H<small>ER</small> husband's laughter had a far more disturbing effect on Georgina than had Wexford's tidings. Something had been slumbering under her veil of apathy. The laughter brought it to life and it showed in her eyes and her trembling lips as raw terror.

'Don't, Denys, don't. Oh, stop!' She clutched his arm and shook it.

'May we share the joke, sir?' asked Wexford blandly.

Villiers stopped laughing as people can when their laughter doesn't stem from amusement but from some irony they have observed with admiration. He shrugged and then, his face going blank, opened his book once more and began to read where he had left off.

'Mrs Villiers,' said Wexford, 'I want to talk to you again about the events of Tuesday night.'

'But, why?' Her voice was barely under control. ' thought it was all over. I was just beginning to stop think-ing about it and now . . . Oh God, what shall I do?' She stood for a moment, staring wildly at them and then ra from the room.

Villiers smiled a little, apparently at something in hi own book. Aware as he was of the huge vanity of writer Wexford was nevertheless unable to understand how on of them could actually laugh at something he had writte himself.

'I can see I shall have to read this book of yours.'

Villiers lifted his eyes and, again closing his book, kept his fingers inside it to mark the place. He took a copy of *Wordsworth in Love* from a stack on the window-sill and handed it to the chief inspector. 'You can have this if it interests you.' The weary grey eyes met Wexford's and held them.

'Thank you. It will interest me. I'm always willing to be enlightened. For one thing, I'm curious to discover why you've made yourself an authority on Wordsworth.'

'A matter of taste, Mr Wexford.'

'But there is always something to account for taste.'

Villiers shrugged impatiently. 'Well, you've brought us the news and we've had our little bit of literary chit-chat. Is there anything else?'

'Certainly there is. I am investigating a murder, Mr Villiers.'

'But not very fruitfully, if I may say so.' Villiers sat down astride a dining chair, his chest against its bars and his arms folded on the top of its back. The ashen face with its tracery of lines again gave Wexford the impression that this man was sick, was dying. 'And what's the point, anyway?' he said. 'Elizabeth is dead and cannot be resurrected. You find who killed her and put him in prison for twenty or thirty years. Who benefits? Who's the happier for it?'

'You're in favour of capital punishment perhaps? I'm surprised your first wife didn't convert you from that view.'

If Villiers was astonished that Wexford knew of his previous marriage he gave no sign of it. 'Capital punishment?' he said. 'No, I'm not in favour of it. I don't care much. I don't care about people being kept in prison

131

either except that my tax pays for their board.'

'It seems to me, sir, that you don't care much for anything.'

'That's so. So-called current affairs don't interest me and nor does current opinion. I don't like people and people don't like me. They're mostly fools,' said the misanthropist with a kind of bitter relish. 'I don't suffer fools gladly. Progress bores me and so does noise.' He added very quietly, 'I want to be left in peace to live in the past.'

'Then let's discuss the past,' said Wexford. 'The recent past. Tuesday night, for instance.'

Sitting opposite Burden in the living room, Georgina said fretfully, 'I told you about Tuesday night last time you were here. If you've got a bad memory you ought to have written it down.'

'Never mind my memory, Mrs Villiers. You just tell me again. You left the Manor at ten-thirty in your husband's car. Who was driving?'

'My husband was driving. He always drives when we're out together. I think the man should always drive, don't you?' She set her mouth stubbornly. 'The man should always be the dominant partner in a marriage so that his wife can look up to him. We,' she said in a loud defiant voice, 'are very happily married.'

'That's nice,' said Burden. 'What time did you reach home?'

'I *told* you. About twenty to eleven. We went in and we went straight to bed. And that's all.'

'No, it isn't all. No one comes home from an evening out and goes straight to bed. One of you must have put the car away. One of you must have locked up.'

'Oh, well, if *that's* what you want. My husband just left the car on the drive. Mine was in the garage.'

'Did you both go into the house together?'

'Of course.'

'Side by side? Squeezing through the door at the same time?'

'Don't be silly,' said Georgina petulantly. 'I went in first and then my husband followed about a minute later. He locked the car because it was going to be left on the drive all night. He always does that.'

'Very prudent. Since you're evidently so careful, you wouldn't have put the milk bottles out before you went to the Manor. Who did that when you got home? Who checked that all the windows were closed and the back door locked?'

She hesitated, looking at him sullenly. Her fingers played nervously with her beads. 'My husband always does that,' she said. 'I went to bed first.'

'How long did it take you to get to bed, Mrs Villiers? Ten minutes? A quarter of an hour? You didn't go to bed unwashed and in all your clothes.'

'Of course I didn't. I put the bedroom light on and undressed and went to the bathroom and then I went to bed. My husband came to bed. He always reads for about half an hour before we go to sleep.'

'Double bed, Mrs Villiers?'

'No, we have twin beds. But you needn't read anything into that. We're a very happy couple.'

'Yes, you told me before. Now, tell me, what time did you go to the Manor?'

'We got there at about half past eight.'

'I believe,' said Burden disarmingly, 'that you often went there to play bridge. How long did you usually stay there?'

'Sometimes till midnight in the holidays.'

'Tuesday night was still in the holidays, wasn't it? Why did you leave so early?'

'My husband,' said Georgina, putting as she always did a self-conscious pride of ownership into the word, 'my husband had some research to do down at the school and . . .' She clapped her hand over her mouth but too late to stifle a little sharp cry. 'When we got home,' she stammered, 'he changed his mind and . . . Oh, why won't you leave us alone? We could be happy if everyone would leave us alone!'

Burden's stare was hard and penetrating. He looked at her without blinking as she began to cry.

'I left the car on the drive,' said Villiers to Wexford. 'No, I didn't check the back door or the windows. That's my wife's province. I went straight to bed and straight to sleep.'

Burden came in. 'May I, sir?'

'Go ahead,' said Wexford.

'What about this research you were going to do down at the school, sir? The essential research that took you away from the Manor at ten-thirty?'

Villiers lit a cigarette. 'Don't you ever make excuses to get away from a boring host and hostess, Inspector?' he asked imperturbably. 'Don't you ever say you're expecting a phone call or you must get back to that boy of yours?'

Burden scowled at him, furious that John had been brought into this interrogation. It was humiliating to find that Villiers, who ostentatiously ignored him as a private person, should all the time have recognised him as a parent.

'So this was an empty excuse,' he said angrily. 'A deliberate lie.'

'Sometimes I do tell lies,' said Villiers, smoking with a kind of frivolous delicacy. 'I'm a good liar.'

'Strange for a man who declares himself indifferent to the opinions of others,' Wexford commented, and suddenly, meeting Villiers' arrogant eyes, a couplet came into his head. He quoted it, not only because it was apt but because he felt a pressing unquenchable need to show Villiers that he wasn't a moron, that he wasn't the flat-footed unlettered country policeman the writer thought him.

' "So much he soared beyond or sunk beneath
The men with whom he felt condemned to breathe." '

The effect was astonishing, not at all what he had expected. Villiers didn't move but his face became feverishly pale. Statue-still, he seemed to be waiting, and not, Wexford thought, for more words, but for action, for some decisive crucial move. And then, perhaps because no one moved but both policemen stood in bewilderment, Villiers laughed.

That laughter electrified Burden into rage.

'What *do* you want, Mr Villiers?' he almost shouted. 'What are you trying to prove? Why do you try to set yourself so much above everyone else?'

'Or beneath them, Mr Burden.' Villiers hadn't shifted his eyes from Wexford's face and now they were very wide and very opaque. 'Or sunk beneath them, remember. As to what I want, that's simple.' He got up, turned his back. 'I want to die,' he said.

'And what the hell,' said Wexford thoughtfully as they got back into the car, 'came over him when I quoted those lines?'

'Search me,' said Burden, the Philistine. He made an effort. 'Er—where do they come from? Wordsworth?'

'I don't think so. I don't know where they come from. They were just sort of floating about in my head.' Burden nodded indifferently. He was used to hearing lines that floated about in his superior's head. Tedious bookishness, that's what it was, and it rather embarrassed him. 'But I'd like to know,' said Wexford. 'It'd be a job tracing them, our England being a nest of singing birds.'

'We've got more important things to worry about,' Burden said impatiently. 'What's more to the point is, are we going to be able to find a witness to corroborate that he didn't go out again after he got home?'

'Or that she didn't.'

'Pity the place is so isolated.'

'Yes. We need to find someone who passed the place in a car. That can wait till the morning. You get that scarf sent over to the lab and then you can get off home to your painting. Manual work often helps the brain, Mike, and you can have a good think while you're wielding the brush.'

With a sigh of relief, Burden started the car. 'Which of those two have you in mind, anyway?'

'Mike, you'll say I'm jumping to conclusions, but I'm as near as dammit certain she did it. She's a strong healthy young woman, physically capable of felling another woman with a torch. It is she and not her husband who inherits. She was at the Manor when the torch was replaced. She knew the layout of the Manor grounds and she could have noticed the bonfire earlier in the evening. If she got blood on her clothes, she knew she could have burnt her outer clothes—say a sweater—on the fire.'

'All this,' said Burden, 'argues premeditation, that she

leliberately chose a torch of all things for her weapon.'

'Think about it. Try and see what you can make of it
ll. I'm going to pick up Lionel Marriott and take him to
he Olive for a drink.'

12

THE new cocktail bar at the Olive and Dove was almost deserted, for by now most of its patrons had deserted it for the dining room, while the serious drinkers were in the public or the saloon. Wexford shepherded Marriott into a secluded corner and placed a large whisky in front of him. The bar communicated with the dining room by means of double glass doors, but Wexford had made sure the diners were out of Marriott's line of vision. He wanted their talk to be uninterrupted and Marriott removed from the temptation of waving to friends or sending smiling dumb-show messages to pretty women.

'Now,' he said, 'I want to hear about this holiday on the Costa Brava.'

'Holiday!' said Marriott, momentarily closing his eyes. 'Really, I'd rather spend a fortnight in a labour camp. The spotty devils are bad enough when you have to cart them up to London to the V. and A., but imagine two weeks cooped up with them in some torrid slum. They go mad, you know. None of the local girls is safe. They're all in an advanced state of satyriasis at the best of times, and once get them in the sun . . . ! And as for appalling infringement of the exchange regulations, you wouldn't believe the diabolical ingenuity of some of them. Every one an accomplished smuggler and his mother's milk scarce out of him.'

'All right, all right,' said Wexford, laughing. 'What about Villiers?'

'God knows how he found the time to go courting. You'd have thought every minute would have been taken up, what with having to be a Customs officer and a male nurse and a watch committee all rolled into one. Anyway, he met Georgina.'

'She was holidaying there too?'

'Only in the same sense that he was,' said Marriott, waving enthusiastically as a satin-gowned brunette swept past their table. Wistfully, he watched her disappear into the dining room. 'Georgina had gone with her own school party,' he said, 'a bunch of teenage nymphomaniacs, from what I heard. Denys and she encountered each other on one of their nightly rounds of the local taverns, picking their charges up off the floor, you know.'

'It really can't have been as bad as that, Lionel.'

'Perhaps I exaggerate a little,' said Marriott airily. 'Not that I heard any of this from Denys. He didn't even bother to send me a card. No, the first hint I got was on the day before he was due back. Elizabeth and Quen dropped in one evening. "We've got some good news for you," said Quen. "Denys has met a girl and they're going to be married." "Fast worker," I said, and then of course I had to say I was pleased, although I was thinking she must be out of her mind, poor thing. Let me get you another drink, Reg.'

'Tonight,' said Wexford firmly, 'I'm the host.' Once let Marriott get to the bar and he would be within range of the allurements of his friends. He asked for two more whiskies and, while he waited for them, he cast his eyes speculatively over the waiters in the dining room, wondering which of them was Quentin Nightingale's rival.

The tall one with acne? The thin youth with slicked-back black hair?

'They were married,' Marriott went on, 'from Georgina's home in Dorset. Quen went down for the wedding but Elizabeth couldn't. She had a migraine. Of course, even Denys couldn't very well bring a second bride home to a horsemeat shop, so Elizabeth asked them to stay at the Manor while they were looking for a house.'

'The Nightingales gave a dinner party for the bride. Everybody who was anybody was there. Old Priscilla and Sir George, the Rogerses from Pomfret, the Primeros from Forby and, of course, your humble servant.' Looking anything but humble, Marriott lowered his voice to a suspenseful whisper. 'Georgina was staying in the house but she was the last to arrive. Ah ha! I thought, making an entrance, the clever little thing. None of us had seen her, so naturally we sat with bated breath. All the women were got up to the nines. Elizabeth looked wonderful. White velvet, you know. It always does something for a woman. Believe it or not, I even saw Denys looking at her with a sort of grudging admiration.

'Then, just when we can contain our impatience no longer, in comes Georgina in Woolworth's pearls and a— well, we used to call them tub frocks, and this one had been in the tub a good many times, I can tell you. Did those women stare! Georgina wasn't a bit shy. In fact, she dominated the conversation at the table. We heard all about her little housewifely plans and how she was going to make a real home for Denys and how they were going to have six children. And possessive! My dear, she actually grumbled to Elizabeth because she hadn't been placed next to him.

'I must say Elizabeth was charming to her. She even complimented her on her dress and really tried to keep her the centre of attention. She was bubbling over with gaiety and she didn't look a day over twenty-five.'

'Georgina,' said Wexford, 'did she seem envious?'

'Of the *mise en scene*? If denigrating everything around one and trying to assume an ascendancy on the grounds of one's middle-class ideas is only a mask for envy, yes, I suppose she was envious. Of course, I've seen her dozens of times since then and all she can talk about is what a marvellous marriage she and Denys have and how they're all in all to each other.'

'And are they?'

'He's everything she wants,' said Marriott, 'although we see no sign of these six children, do we? As for him, I think he's as bored with his second marriage as he was with his first, but there's only one thing that interests Denys Villiers and that's his work. Once he and Georgina were settled in their bungalow, he was buzzing round the Manor again just like the old days.'

Wexford said slyly, 'You must have been buzzing too to have seen him there.'

For a moment Marriott looked a little foolish. Then he jumped up smartly. 'You'll excuse me one second while I pop into the dining room and have a word with . . .'

Wexford laughed. 'I'll excuse you altogether,' he said, for tonight.'

'You've been thinking,' said Dr Crocker on the following morning, 'that she was wearing that scarf when the deed was done. Well, she wasn't. It would have been saturated with blood if she had.'

'Perhaps it was round her neck or she was holding it in her hand.'

The doctor gave a derisive snort. 'And after she was dead she took it off and wiped her head with it? That's what it looks as if it was used for, to wipe blood off someone or something.'

Wexford folded the report and put it down on his blotter. 'You said you were out delivering a baby on Tuesday night,' he said. 'I don't suppose your route took you through Myfleet via Clusterwell?'

'Sure it did. Why?'

'You know Villiers' bungalow?'

'Of course I do. He's a patient of mine. I passed it at about eleven.'

'Did you notice the bungalow at all?' Wexford said more urgently. 'Were any lights on? Were the cars on the drive?'

The doctor's face fell. 'I didn't look. I was thinking about my patient and the possibility of the child being a breech presentation. Now, if I'd known . . .'

'That,' said Wexford irritably, 'is what they all say. Here's Mike now.'

Burden came in wearily. 'Three of us have done a house-to-house in Myfleet,' he said. 'I don't reckon any of them go out in the evenings. The whole place shuts up about nine and those that aren't in bed are in the pub. Nobody passed that way bar Katje Doorn. I've talked to her again and all she did was simper and tell me about a disgusting Swedish film. Though I did have the feeling she didn't want to discuss her drive.'

Wexford gave a slight embarrassed cough. 'Rubbish,' he said, listening to the bluster in his voice and trying to quell it. 'I tell you, that girl had nothing to do with Mrs Nightingale's death.'

'Perhaps not. But it's a bit funny, isn't it? She'll talk very freely about her goings-on with Nightingale and that waiter, but she shuts up like a clam when I try to get her to describe her drive home. And another thing, Nightingale's Mini was standing out by those stables and young Lovell was cleaning it, doing his best to get a scratch off the front bumper.'

'I don't know where all this is getting us, Mike. We aren't looking for a damaged car but for a witness who saw something when he passed Villiers' bungalow.'

'I like all the ends tidied,' said Burden. 'Anyway, I checked downstairs and no accident was reported on Tuesday night.'

'Then let's leave it, shall we?' said Wexford crossly. 'Get Martin to go over to Clusterwell and find out if anyone does any regular nightly dog walking. I may as well go myself,' he added. 'Spy out the land a bit. It's not possible *no one* used that road.'

The cottages of Clusterwell were scattered over a spider-shaped network of lanes. Sergeant Martin took the body of the spider, Wexford its legs. Recalling the painstaking routine work of his youth, he knocked on every door. But the inhabitants of Clusterwell took a perverse pride in their own peculiar brand of respectability. Like those of Myfleet, they stayed in at night. Virtue lay in bolting one's doors, drawing one's curtains and gathering round the television by nine o'clock. And, judging by the number of mongrels Wexford encountered in the lanes, their dogs exercised themselves.

A large black one, patrolling what looked like a field of allotments, growled at him as he approached the hedge. He decided to venture no nearer the caravan—in any case clearly deserted—which stood behind runner-bean vines and stacked chicken coops. Instead he stepped back to read the words on a shabby board mounted on poles: *A. Tawney. New-laid eggs, roasting chickens, veg.*

'Myfleet,' he said tersely to his driver.

Mrs Cantrip was in her rocking chair, engrossed in her

paper, a little flustered because he had caught her in idleness. Katje, who had shown him in, disappeared in the
direction of the study.

'Alf Tawney, sir? If he's not out on his rounds, you'll
likely find him over at Mrs Lovell's.'

'How does he travel to and fro?'

'On his bike, sir. He's got one of them big baskets on
the handlebars of his bike.'

Wexford nodded. 'Does he stay at Mrs Lovell's all
night?'

It was easy to shock Mrs Cantrip, who adhered to that
school of thought which holds that fornication can only
be committed between midnight and dawn. 'Oh no, sir,'
she said, flushing and looking down. 'He's always gone by
eleven. I reckon even Mrs Lovell's got some idea of what's
right.'

The lovers were in the middle of their evening meal. A
saucepan of baked beans stood in the middle of the cloth-
less table.

Mrs Lovell re-seated herself. 'His lordship been up to
something?' she asked, carving more bread and resting
her gigantic bosom among the crumbs.

'My visit has nothing to do with Sean.' It was clear to
Wexford that he was to be offered no tea, but a glance at
the cracked cups and the scum-ringed milk bottle told
him he wasn't missing anything. 'I hoped to have the
pleasure of a little talk with Mr Tawney.'

'With Alf? What d'you want with Alf?'

Wexford eyed the purveyor of eggs and vegetables,
wondering how to interrogate a man who apparently
never opened his mouth. The small black eyes in the
swarthy hatchet face stared expressionlessly back at him.

144

At last he said, 'Spend a good deal of time here with our friends, do you, Mr Tawney?'

Mrs Lovell gave a full-throated giggle. 'My Sean's no friend of his,' she said. 'It's me you come to see, don't you, Alf?'

'Um,' said Tawney lugubriously.

'And very nice too,' said Wexford. 'A man needs a little feminine company after a hard day's work.'

'And his hot meals. Wasting away Alf was till I got him coming here. You fancy a cream horn, Alf?'

'Um.'

'What time,' said Wexford, 'do you reckon on leaving Mrs Lovell's to go home?'

'Alf has to be up betimes,' said Mrs Lovell, looking more gypsy-ish than ever. 'He's always gone by a quarter to eleven.' She sighed and Wexford guessed that this early retreat had been a bone of contention between them in the past. With surprising intelligence, she said, 'You want to know if he saw anything the night her up at the Manor got killed?'

'Precisely. I want to know if Mr Tawney took a look at Mr Villiers' bungalow—you know the one I mean?— as he was cycling back to Clusterwell.'

'Don't know about look. He tried to knock them up, didn't you, Alf?'

'Um,' said Tawney. Very alert now, Wexford waited.

'Go on, Alf. The gentleman asked you a question.' A tremor disturbed Tawney's body as if, by unprecedented effort, he was trying to summon speech from the depths of his stomach. 'He was mad enough about it at the time,' said Mrs Lovell. 'Quite talkative for him. *Go on*, Alf.'

Tawney spoke.

' 'Twere no good,' he said. 'They was out and the place locked up.'

'Now let's get this straight,' said Wexford, guessing for all he was worth and mentally apologising to Burden. 'Mr Tawney was riding home when a car passed him and nearly knocked him off his bicycle.' Mrs Lovell's admiring grin told him he was guessing right. 'And he took the number of this car, intending to give it to the police so that the driver might be prosecuted.'

'He never took the number.' Mrs Lovell dipped into a paper bag for the last cream horn. 'He knew who it was. That foreign girl from the Manor.'

'Mr Tawney knocked at the bungalow because he wanted to use their phone?' Incredible to imagine Tawney explaining, apologising, dialling, explaining again.

'The place was all dark,' said Mrs Lovell with relish, the gypsy scaring children with her stories round the camp fire. 'Alf banged and banged, but no one come, did they?'

'Nope,' said Tawney.

Talk about hearsay evidence, thought Wexford. 'What time was it?'

'Alf left here half past ten. He'd been knocking a long time when the clock struck eleven, Clusterwell church clock. Go on, Alf, you tell him. You was there.'

Tawney swigged his last drop of tea, perhaps to lubricate his rarely used vocal cords. 'I banged and no one come.' He coughed horribly and Wexford looked away. 'He's out and she's out, I said to myself.'

'That's right, Alf.' Mrs Lovell beamed encouragement.

'Might have known. The garage doors was open.'

'And both cars was gone! So Alf give it up, and next morning—well, you cool off, don't you? You think to yourself, Why bother when there's no bones broken. Mind you, I'll let that little foreign bitch know what I know if I see her about the village.'

Poor Katje. Wexford wondered if he should drop her a gentle word of warning, closeted with her, calling her by her Christian name, even though that privilege had only been accorded him because he reminded her of some old uncle. Talk to her like an old Dutch uncle . . . ? He laughed to himself. Better forget it, stay securely tied to the mast while the siren sang for others.

In September even the best-kept gardens usually have a ripe wild look. This one was a barren island among the fields, a sterile characterless plot in which every unruly branch and every straggling stem had been docked. The grass was brown and closely shorn and there was nothing to provide shade.

Denys and Georgina Villiers sat in a pair of deckchairs, the uncomfortable cheap kind which have thin metal frames and economically small wooden arm-rests. Wexford observed them for a moment before making his presence known. The man who said he never read newspapers was reading one now, apparently oblivious of his wife. With neither book nor sewing to occupy her, she stared at him with the rapt attention of a cinema fanatic gazing at the screen.

Wexford coughed and immediately Georgina sprang to her feet. Villiers looked up and said with the icy unpleasantness he seemed always able to muster, 'Control yourself. Don't be so silly.'

Wexford walked up to them. Over Villiers' shoulder he looked at the newspaper and saw what he had been reading: a review of his own latest published work which occupied half a page. 'Mr Villiers,' he said roughly, 'why did you tell me you came straight home from the Manor on Tuesday night and went to bed? This house was empty and in darkness at eleven. Why didn't you tell me you went out again?'

'I forgot,' said Villiers calmly.

'You *forgot*? When I asked you most pointedly?'

'Nevertheless, I forgot.' Villiers' cold face showed neither fear nor embarrassment. The man had a curious strength, an iron self-control; he seemed unbreakable. Why then have this strange sensation that he had been irrevocably broken long ago and that his strength had never been quite strong enough?

'Come now, sir. You forgot you went out. Very well. Have you also forgotten where you went?'

'I went,' said Villiers, 'where I said I was going, to the school library to look up a reference.'

'What reference?'

With cool contempt, Villiers said, 'Would it mean anything to you if I told you?' He shrugged. 'All right. I was looking up the precise relationship of George Gordon Wordsworth to William Wordsworth.'

Somewhat to his own humiliation, Wexford found that it did indeed mean nothing. He swung round on Georgina who crouched in her deckchair, gooseflesh on her arms and tiny beads of sweat on her upper lip. For once she wore no jewellery. Did the cheap gaudy stuff no longer please her now that she would be able to adorn herself with real gems? Or had she ferreted out of Nightingale the scornful words in which her sister-in-law's bequest was couched?

'Did you accompany your husband to the school, Mrs Villiers?' He noted the faint shake of her head. 'Had you done so you would hardly have gone in two separate cars. But you went out. Where?'

Her voice came in a shrill squeak. 'I drove—I drove around the lanes.'

'May I ask why?'

Villiers answered for her. 'My wife,' he said silkily, 'was annoyed with me for going out. She did what she often does on such occasions, took her own car and went for a country drive.' He gave a waspish smile. 'To cool her temper,' he said.

'I'm not convinced of any of this,' said Wexford slowly. He glanced around the bare garden. 'I think we could all talk more frankly down at the police station.'

Georgina gave a wild cry and threw herself into her husband's arms. Wexford expected him to repudiate her but instead he held her with almost a lover's tenderness. Standing up now, he stroked her dry rough hair. 'As you like,' he said indifferently.

'No, no, no,' she sobbed into his shoulder. 'You must tell him. You tell him.'

He was going to lie again. Wexford was sure of it.

'What my wife wants me to tell you,' said Villiers, 'is that you've been a complete bloody fool.' He patted Georgina as one pats a dog and then he pushed her away. 'Let me give you a piece of advice, Chief Inspector. Next time you suspect anyone of murder for gain, you had better check up on the value of what they're gaining. I'm a good liar,' he said urbanely, 'but I'm not lying now. My sister's pieces of jewellery are all fakes. I'd be surprised if the whole lot would fetch more than fifty pounds. You had better look elsewhere, Mr Wexford. You know as well as I do that your absurd trumped-up case against my wife has nothing but motive to make it stand up, and where is your motive now?'

Gone with the sun, thought Wexford, watching it sink behind the misty fields. He was suddenly quite sure that this time Villiers hadn't been lying.

13

KATJE was nowhere to be seen and it was Quentin Nightingale himself who this time admitted Wexford to the Manor. But Wexford sensed her recent presence in the austere study. He felt that she had been standing here with Quentin, in his arms, kissing him, then running away when the bell rang.

Quentin himself had an abstracted air, the look of a lover dreaming of the past, impatient for the near future. Wexford's news jolted him into unwelcome reality.

'Every piece of jewellery Elizabeth had I bought for her,' he said. 'I've still got the receipts for most of it, if you'd care to see them.'

'Later. First I should like to see the stones themselves again.'

Quentin removed the Stubbs, opened the safe. Then he lifted the jewels from their boxes in handfuls, letting them fall through his fingers, as a child on its first visit to the seaside sifts shells and stones, its pleasure mixed with astonishment at the unknown.

He picked out from the heap his dead wife's engagement ring and took it to the window, but the growing dusk defeated him and, returning, he switched on the desk lamp.

'My glasses,' he said. 'Just by your elbow. Would you mind?'

Wexford handed them to him.

'This is a fake.' There was a small quiver in Quentin's voice. 'This isn't the ring I gave Elizabeth on our engagement.'

'How do you know?'

'Not because I'm an expert on precious stones. I shall have to find an expert to tell us for sure about the rest. Are there any to be found around here or should I get someone down from London?'

'We can find someone here. You haven't told me how you know that ring is false.'

Quentin said bitterly, 'When I bought it for her I had some words engraved inside it.' Taking the ring from him, Wexford knew he wasn't going to be told what those words had been. 'There's nothing inside this one.'

'No.'

Quentin sat down. With a rapid, almost reflex gesture, he pushed the sparkling heap away from him, knocking a rivière of diamonds—diamonds or paste?—on to the carpet. It lay like a glittering snake at Wexford's feet.

'I suppose,' Quentin said, 'that they're all copies. Perfect copies too, aren't they? All but one. Exquisite facsimiles of the real thing. Except one. She had the stone copied and the platinum copied but she didn't bother to have the words copied because they meant nothing to her. How utterly indifferent she must have been to me. . . .'

Was it this indifference, finally and irrevocably brought home to him, that made Quentin's mind up for him? Was it this knowledge that led him to take his new and perhaps reckless step? Much later, after the case was over, Wexford often asked himself these questions. But on the following morning, returning to the Manor from the jeweller's, he hadn't given them a moment's thought and the news came to him as a complete surprise.

Katje showed him into the drawing room and he was already unwrapping the brown paper from the jewel boxes as he followed her when he saw that Quentin wasn't alone. Denys Villiers was with him, standing by the french windows and holding both Quentin's hands in his. Wexford heard the tail end of what sounded like a speech.

'. . . Anyway, my best congratulations, Quen. I couldn't be more glad for you.' Then Villiers saw Wexford. He dropped his brother-in-law's hands and his face set arrogantly.

'May I know what ground there is for congratulation, sir?'

Villiers shrugged and turned his back, but Quentin, flushing, put out a hand to Katje and the girl ran to him.

'Perhaps I'm indiscreet to tell you, Chief Inspector. You might read so much into this.' Villiers made a faint derisive sound. 'I'd like it kept secret for the time being,' Quentin said. 'Katje and I are going to be married.'

Wexford put down his parcel. 'Indeed?' he said. They looked like father and daughter standing there. There was even a slight resemblance between them, the family likeness apparent between any two people belonging to the classic north European type. 'Then let me congratulate you also,' he said, and again he apologised silently to Burden, whose ideas had perhaps been not so old fashioned after all.

'Naturally, we shall wait six months. A year might be more . . .'

'But I am not waiting a whole year, Kventin. Half a year perhaps. It is not fair if you are making me wait a whole year for my flat in London and my new fast sports car and my going all round the world for my honeymoon.'

So she was a gold-digger, after all. Wexford though

dly. He had been wrong. These days it seemed that he
as always wrong.

'Now I should like to see you alone, sir,' he said.

'Yes, of course.'

Abruptly Villiers threw open the french windows and
alked out of the room. Casting a dazzling smile over her
oulder, Katje followed him to pause on the lawn and
rvey everything around her with frank concupiscence.

'She'll go home to her parents until the wedding,'
entin said, and earnestly, 'I want everything to be
ht. I want—what is it Antony says? "Read not my
mishes in the world's report. I have not kept my
are."'

'"But that to come,"' Wexford capped it, '"shall all be
ne by the rule."' I daresay, he thought, I daresay. But
at of 'that to come' for her? Such a long future, so
ch money, such idleness for temptations to gain ground
She was the last for him and he perhaps only one of
first for her. Would they dine at the Olive sometimes
d be served by a waiter who had once romped with
s lady of the Manor in the coverts of Cheriton Forest?
or Kventin, Wexford thought, aping her accent. He
s no longer to be envied. It was a nice game he was
ying, a game which had once seemed enticing to Wex-
d. But not any more, not on those terms, for it wasn't
rth the exorbitant price of the candle.

'The jewellery,' he said laconically, 'is all fake. I took
to an old jeweller in Queen Street. He's helped me in
past and he's absolutely reliable. If he says it's fake,
fake. She must have sold what you bought her and
exact copies made.'

'But why, Chief Inspector? I gave her all the money
could possibly have needed. If she wanted more she
only to ask. She knew that.'

153

'Would you have given her thirty thousand pounds?'

'I'm not a millionaire, Mr Wexford.' Quentin sighed, bit his lip. 'The jewellery was hers to do as she liked with. She chose to sell it. Perhaps it doesn't matter why.' He met Wexford's eyes pleadingly. 'I'd like to forget the whole thing.'

'It isn't as simple as that.' Wexford sat down, rather imperiously motioning his host to sit down too. 'Your wife sold her jewellery because she needed money. Now it's my turn to ask why. Why did she need money, Mr Nightingale, and what did she do with it? We know she spent it. Her bank account was overdrawn. Where did the money go?'

Quentin shrugged unhappily. 'She was generous. Perhaps she gave it to charity.'

'Thirty thousand pounds? And why keep it dark from you? No, Mr Nightingale, I think your wife was blackmailed.'

Quentin leaned forward, frowning his bewilderment. 'But that's impossible! People are only blackmailed when they've done something against the law. My wife was . . .' He waved a helpless hand, encompassing the room. Wexford understood what he was trying to put into words, that the woman who had reigned here had been entirely cushioned by her position and her wealth from the squalor of criminal temptation. We aren't of that class, his eyes said, of that seamy underworld. Haven't you realised yet that we are only a little lower than the angels?

'It need not necessarily have been some offence against the law,' said Wexford quietly, 'but against morality.'

Puzzled, Quentin seemed to consider. Then his brow cleared. 'You mean she might have been unfaithful to me and someone found it out?'

'Something of that kind, sir.'

'No, Mr Wexford, you're on the wrong track. I wasn't that kind of husband either. Whatever my wife had done would have forgiven her, and she knew it. We discussed the subject soon after we were married, as young couples do. Elizabeth asked me for my views. It was an academic question, you understand, a matter of seeking to know me better. We were—we were very much in love in those days.'

'And what was your answer?'

'That if she ever came to me and told me she had—that there had been someone else, I would never blame her, certainly not divorce her. Not as long as she came to me and confided in me. I told her that I believed forgiveness to be a part of love, and that in such circumstances, when she was unhappy, she would need me most. And I would expect her to do the same by me if the need arose. I would never have divorced her. She was my wife, and even when we grew so terribly apart I still believed that marriage was for ever.'

A nice man, Wexford thought, his usual cynicism for a moment in abeyance, a kind and eminently civilised person. Cynicism returned. An ideal husband, or a man fate had designed for women to take for a ride? It was, he reflected, a good thing Quentin Nightingale had formed such admirable principles during his first marriage as he would certainly have to put them into practice during his second.

'There are some things,' he said, 'which cannot be forgiven.' Illustrations came into his mind, examples from his long experience of wrongdoers. There was the woman who had taken her husband back a dozen times after his terms of imprisonment for theft, but had refused ever to see him again when he had been convicted for indecent exposure. Or the man who had borne his wife's infidelity

for twenty years but when she was caught shoplifting had
repudiated her. 'You're an intelligent broad-minded man,'
he said at last, 'but you're very conventional. I wonder if
you really know yourself. You know what pleases you
but do you know what would disgust you?'

'Nothing Elizabeth could have done,' Quentin said
obstinately.

'Perhaps not, but she believed it would have disgusted
you, believed it so firmly that she was prepared to pay
thirty thousand pounds to keep it from you.'

'If you say so,' Quentin said helplessly. 'Who could she
ever have known that would extort money from her?'

'I was hoping you could tell me that. A servant?'

'Mrs Cantrip who has been devoted to us for sixteen
years? Old Will who is respect itself? Sean who wor-
shipped the very ground she walked on? You see yourself
how absurd this is. Why should it be a servant, anyway?'

'It's more unlikely that it was one of her friends, isn't
it, sir? A servant who lived in this house would have
access to private papers, might have been an eye witness,
might have discovered photographs.'

'Evidence of infidelity? I tell you, she *knew* I'd have
understood. I'd have overlooked it, however much it
hurt.'

Wexford stared at him, hardly able to contain his
impatience. The man didn't know what life was. He spoke
of infidelity as if it was always a straightforward and
temporary preference for someone else, a matter of
temptation, of love and of subsequent guilt. He was innocent. But Wexford wasn't. He had seen the letters even
the most elevated and cultured lovers write to each other,
the photographs elegant and fastidious women revel in
posing for. Thirty thousand pounds might not be too great
a price to pay to keep them from a husband's eye.

'You had a series of *au pair* girls, you told me.'

'Ordinary young girls,' Quentin said. 'Quite straight-forward and happy to be here. They adored Elizabeth.'

Just like Katje did?

'Before the girls came,' said Wexford, 'you had a married couple. What was the name again?'

'Twohey,' said Quentin Nightingale.

The small white cottage was being scoured from top to bottom. When Wexford arrived, Mrs Cantrip abandoned the cleaning that had necessarily to be done on a Saturday, and sat down with the ginger cat in her lap. The room smelt strongly of polish and mothballs.

'Twohey, sir?' she said. 'Mr Nightingale dismissed him for insolence. He never showed a proper respect, not from the start, and he never did a fair day's work, as far as I could see. Always hanging about where he wasn't sup-posed to be, snooping and listening, if you know what I mean.'

'And that was why he was sacked?'

The cat slithered to the floor and began sharpening its claws against a table leg. 'Stop that, Ginger,' said Mrs Cantrip. 'Well, things came to a head, sir, and that's a fact. A couple of weeks before he was sacked he got so disrespectful to Madam it was past bearing, and Madam always so gentle and never standing up for herself.' She picked up the cat and dropped it out of the window among the zinnias and dahlias. 'She caught him helping himself to Mr Nightingale's whisky, and when she spoke to him about it, he said, "There's plenty more where that came from," if you've ever heard the like.'

'And his wife?'

'She wasn't so bad. Under his thumb, if the truth were known. She took quite a fancy to me. Sent me a Christmas card two years running.'

'You know their address, then?' Wexford asked urgently.

'I never wrote back, sir,' said Mrs Cantrip, bristling a little with indignation. 'They weren't the kind of folks I'd care to associate with. I did notice the first one had a Newcastle postmark.'

'Did they continue in service?'

'That I wouldn't know, sir. Twohey was always bragging and boasting, and he did say he was sick of the life. Going to set himself up in a hardware business, he said, but Mrs Twohey said to me, out of his hearing like, that it was all castles in the air. Where would they get the capital, sir? They hadn't a penny to bless themselves and that's a fact.'

Having left Sergeant Martin to begin the search for Twohey, Wexford drove down Tabard Road and parked in front of a bungalow whose pink front door matched the geraniums in its garden. Two children sat on a ground sheet on the lawn, but at opposite ends of it, as if they had put as much space between them as was consistent with their mother's rule about not sitting on damp grass. The boy was cleaning paint brushes, the girl transferring caterpillars from a glass jar into a collection of match boxes.

Wexford greeted them cheerfully, then strolled up to their father who was painting his garage doors. He noted with an inward chuckle that Burden looked anything but pleased to see him.

'Carry on painting,' said Wexford. 'I like watching other people work. You needn't look so worried. I only want you to lend an ear while I talk.' And he told Burden about the jewellery and about Twohey.

Behind them the children, who had been silent since

Wexford's arrival, began a soft though fierce bickering.

'I was wondering if what this Twohey found out was the secret of Villiers' and Mrs Nightingale's intense dislike of each other. There's no doubt Nightingale is very attached to Villiers, and if he found out his wife had once done her brother some dreadful injury . . .'

'But what dreadful injury, sir?' Burden dipped his brush into the paint, scraping the bottom of the tin. 'Look at my two,' he said bitterly. 'They really seem to hate each other and there's no cause for it, as far as I can see. They've been like cat and dog ever since John was a toddler and Pat in her pram.'

'It'll be different when they're grown up.'

'But will it? Why shouldn't the Villiers-Nightingale case be a parallel? Apparently you get these cases of brothers and sisters who are absolutely incompatible.'

'They were separated,' Wexford said. 'They never had a chance to adjust to each other in the late teens and early twenties. If you separated Pat and John, then they might turn out like Villiers and Elizabeth, because one or other of them might let an old grievance smoulder. Your two will grow more tolerant from daily contact.'

'I don't know,' said Burden. 'Sometimes I think of sending one of them away to boarding school.'

'But you can see that separation doesn't work, Mike.' Wexford sat down on the short stepladder. 'I wonder if it's possible that Twohey killed her himself? If it was he she met in the forest and he killed her when she told him her source of supply had come to an end?'

'Then how,' Burden objected, 'did he get hold of the torch? He was the last person to have access to the garden room at the Manor.'

'True. Now, let's see. Our case against Georgina falls to the ground because now we know Georgina had no

159

motive. Villiers remains a possibility. He could have killed her because, her money having come to an end, she told him she would reveal everything to Nightingale. That bloody secret, whatever it was. Sean could have killed her because he saw her with another man.'

'No, sir. We know it was premeditated. The killer took the torch with him.' Burden placed his brush on his paint rag and turned the now empty tin upside down. 'John!' he called, then, 'John!' more loudly to make his voice heard above the quarrelling. 'Go into the shed, will you, and fetch me another tin of pink?'

'I can't. It's pitch dark in there and the bulb's gone.'

'Well, take a torch, then. Don't be so feeble, and leave your sister's things alone.'

'Encouraging garden pests,' said John scathingly. He got up with a sigh, trailed into the open garage and reached up for a torch which stood on a high shelf.

Wexford watched him, saying slowly, 'Of course. Why didn't I think of it before? We realised almost from the first that when you're going into a place that you know will be dark you take a torch with you. But you take your own torch, don't you? Everyone owns a torch. John knew exactly where his torch was and he fetched it as a matter of course. We've been daft, Mike. We thought of someone going to the Manor and taking the Nightingales' torch. But why should they? What possible purpose could there be in going out of your way in securing a weapon that was the property of the woman you intended to kill? Why not bring your own?'

'But the murderer didn't bring his own,' Burden objected. He struck his forehead with the flat of his hand, leaving a broad pink smear. 'No, I'm being stupid. You mean that, if we exclude Nightingale himself, the only possible person to have taken that torch into the wood was Elizabeth herself?'

'That's what I mean. And you know what else it means? No one would choose a torch as a murder weapon if there was anything else to hand. Therefore, *no one planned this murder*. The killer premeditated nothing. He (or she) was overcome by an impulse of the moment and struck Elizabeth Nightingale with the torch she herself had brought with her.'

Burden nodded gravely. 'She brought it,' he agreed, 'but someone else put it back.'

And, Wexford asked himself, how did Villiers know the jewels were fakes?

14

WEXFORD walked to church with his wife and lef
her at the gate. Without any religious feeling him
self, he sometimes went to morning service to please her
Today his office called him as peremptorily as the churc
bells had called her, but with a silent beckoning finger.

Burden was already there, busy at the phone, setting i
motion the search for Twohey.

'Born in Dublin about fifty years ago,' Wexford hear
him say. 'Dark, Irish-looking, small eyes, cyst at the le
corner of his mouth unless he's had it removed. One co
viction, fraudulent conversion while he was a hote
manager in Manchester in 1954. That's right, could be i
your Newcastle or Newcastle under Lyme. Keep in touch
He put the receiver down and grinned wryly at h
superior.

'You've been doing your homework,' Wexford sai
when Burden handed him a photograph of the man h
had described. 'I thought I told you to take last evenir
off and finish your painting?'

'I have finished it. Anyway, I didn't do my homewo
last night, but I was up bright and early this mornin
I've been having a conference with Mrs Cantrip.'

'Has she any idea how the money was paid over
Twohey?'

Burden closed the window. He didn't care for the sou
of the bells. 'It was all news to her. I don't think she rea

took it in. Her Mrs Nightingale being blackmailed!'

'She'd never heard of such a thing,' said Wexford with a grin, 'and that's a fact?'

'Something like that. She's sure Twohey isn't in the neighbourhood because if he was his wife would have come to see her.'

Wexford shrugged. Burden had planted himself in the solidly built swivel chair, so there was no help for it but to settle for one of the flimsier seats. He glared at the inspector and said coldly, 'Why should he be in the neighbourhood?'

'Because maybe it was him,' Burden said ungrammatically, 'that Mrs Nightingale met in the forest.'

'It's blackmailers that get killed, not their victims.'

'Suppose she told him her source had dried up? He might have killed her in a rage. We know it wasn't premeditated, don't we? Thank goodness those bells have stopped.' He opened the window again, raising the blind so that the sun streamed into Wexford's eyes. Wexford shifted his chair irritably. 'Or Sean Lovell might have seen them together and mistaken the reason for their meeting and . . .'

'So you're coming round to young Lovell yourself now, are you?'

'I've felt differently about him since he told me he took a knife to his mother when he was a young lad and saw her with one of her men. Besides, there's the money he gets. I bet she told him she was leaving him all her money and she might not have said how much. He'd have thought it was a hell of a lot more than it was.'

'Come off it, Mike. He either killed her from jealousy or he killed her for gain. The two don't go together.' Wexford got up. 'Well, I'm off to stand Lionel Marriott a drink in the Olive.'

Burden picked up the phone once more. 'Very nice,' he said distantly. 'I'm sorry I'm too busy to join you.'

'Wait till you're asked,' Wexford snapped. Then he chuckled. ' "Blessed is he," Mike, "that sitteth not in the seat of the scornful." '

'Well, it's your seat, sir,' said Burden blandly.

It was funny the way Burden seemed to have taken over everything these days, Wexford thought as he hung over the Kingsbrook Bridge, waiting for the Olive and Dove to open and for Marriott to come. When he looked back on the past week's investigations it seemed to him that Burden had done most of the enquiries while he had sat listening to Marriott's stories. Perhaps he was exaggerating. But Burden was certainly proving to be right in his theories. About the lack of premeditation, for instance, and Katje wanting to marry Nightingale and Georgina Villiers being just a nice ordinary woman. Soon, no doubt, he would have a theory as to the secret and another to account for Sean's non-existent alibi. He dropped a chipping from the bridge parapet into the water. Our young men shall see visions, he thought, and our old men shall dream dreams. . . .

'A penny for your thoughts,' said Marriott, tapping him on the shoulder.

'I was thinking I'm getting old, Lionel.'

'But you're the same age as I am!'

'A little younger, I think,' said Wexford gently. 'It just struck me, this case is full of people who are too old for other people. It reminds me that I'm older than the lot of them.' He looked up at the serene Sussex sky, cloudless and brilliant. 'An old man in a dry month,' he said. 'An old man on a dry case . . .'

'The Olive won't be dry,' said Marriott. 'Come on, Gerontius, let's have that drink.'

On sunny days the patrons of the Olive could have their drinks at tables in the garden. It was a dusty little garden, rather arid, but Wexford and Marriott, like most Englishmen, felt it almost a duty to sit outside when the sun shone, for fine weather came so seldom and lasted so short a time.

'But I've told you the whole story, Reg,' Marriott said. 'There isn't any more.'

'That from *you*?'

'I'm afraid so, unless you want me to embroider it with my own ideas.'

Wexford picked a leaf out of his drink and looked irritably up into the tree from which it had fallen. He said sharply, 'Do you think it possible that Villiers is homosexual?'

'Oh, my dear, I shouldn't think so.'

'And yet you say he had no women friends between his marriages.'

'He didn't have any men friends either.'

'No? What about Quentin Nightingale?'

'Quentin certainly isn't. I've a shrewd suspicion he's chasing that little Dutch girl. Gone overboard for her, if you ask me. I grant you Denys's feelings for his wives have only been lukewarm, but Quen was in love with Elizabeth when he met her and now he's in love again.'

Wexford wasn't going to betray Nightingale's confidence even by a nod of agreement. 'I wondered,' he said, 'if Elizabeth knew her brother was homosexual and hated him for it but was prepared to go to considerable lengths to keep it dark.'

'I don't see why she'd get murdered for that.'

Finishing his drink, Wexford decided not to breathe a

word to Marriott about the blackmail payments. 'No, it's more likely she was seen in the forest with a man and the person who saw her killed her.' He added thoughtfully, ' "My little songbird, the only true Nightingale in Myfleet." '

In an eager helpful voice, Marriott said, 'Perhaps he's Quen's natural child. Will Palmer's always going about saying "he never had no father". How about that?'

'What have you been reading?' Wexford snapped. 'Mrs Henry Wood? *The Marriage of Figaro?*'

'Sorry. It was just an idea.'

'And a very poor one. You may be a good teacher of English, Lionel, but you're a rotten detective.' Wexford smiled ruefully. 'Even worse than me,' he said, and he got up, wondering what Burden had found out in his absence.

Marriott remained sitting at the table for a moment but he caught Wexford up just as the chief inspector was crossing the bridge.

'I've remembered something,' he said, out of breath. 'Elizabeth used to send a hell of a lot of parcels. Smallish brown-paper parcels. Often, when I've been up there in the daytime, I've seen a parcel on the hall table, but there was always a letter or two waiting for the post on top of it. Any use to you?'

'I don't know, but thanks all the same.'

'You're welcome, my dear,' said Marriott, turning to leave him. He looked back over his shoulder and added rather wistfully, 'Don't drop me, Reg, now you've squeezed me dry.'

'Even a copper needs friends,' said Wexford, and then he walked back up the High Street to the police station.

Burden was sitting at the rosewood desk eating a sandwich lunch.

'Clear out of it,' said Wexford crossly. 'You're making crumbs on my blotter.'

'You always make crumbs.'

'Maybe, but it's my blotter and, incidentally, my office.'

'Sorry, sir,' said Burden virtuously. 'I thought you'd gone on a pub crawl.'

Wexford gave an ill-tempered snort. He blew away the crumbs and sat down with dignity. 'Any news?'

'Not yet. No dice from either of the Newcastles. I've been on to Dublin.'

'You're wrong about one thing, Mike. Twohey didn't meet Mrs Nightingale in any forest. She sent his money to him in parcels. I don't know to what address but we could try asking Katje.'

Burden compressed his lips into a thin line.

'You've had your lunch,' said Wexford, 'so I suggest you get over there now.'

Burden groaned. 'Do I have to?' he said in an almost schoolboy voice, in the voice of his son.

'Are you joking?' Wexford roared. 'Are you out of your mind? She won't eat you.'

'It's not being eaten that I'm scared of,' said Burden. He screwed up his lunch paper, dropped it in the basket and went out, giving Wexford a glance of mock dismay.

There was nothing more for him to do now, Wexford reflected, but wait. He sent Bryant to the canteen to fetch him some lunch and after he had eaten it a great weariness overcame him. He decided to read to keep himself awake and, since the only reading matter he had to hand apart from a heap of reports he knew by heart was the book Denys Villiers had given him, he read that. Or, to put it more accurately, he read the first three paragraphs, only to nod off and nearly jump out of his skin when the phone bell shrilled.

'Try hardware shops,' he told his caller tiredly. 'Especially those which have changed hands in the past four years. He may have changed his name.' With a spark of inspiration, he added, 'I'd be interested in any ironmonger's shop called Nightingale's or, say, the Manor Stores.'

He returned to page one of *Wordsworth in Love*, flicked on to a family tree. There, in strong black type, was the name, George Gordon Wordsworth. He had been, Wexford noted, the poet's own grandson. And this piece of information, already recorded in his newly published book, was what Villiers had led him to believe he had sought from the school library. The man had a weakness, then, the weakness of underrating his opponent.

It was nearly six before Burden got back.

'My God, you've been long enough.'

'She and Nightingale were out. Picnicking, I gather. I waited till they got back.'

'Could she remember the address on the parcels?'

'She says she only posted parcels of stuff Mrs Nightingale sent to Holland, except for last Tuesday, the day Mrs N. got killed. Then she posted two, one to her mother in Holland and another one. She never even looked at the address.'

Wexford shrugged. 'Well, it was worth a try, Mike. Sorry about your Sunday afternoon. I don't suppose you met with a fate worse than death, though, did you?'

'Nightingale was there all the time.'

'You make him sound,' said Wexford, 'like a nurse in a doctor's consulting room. Well, I'm going to Myfleet myself now just for another scout round that forest and maybe a talk with Mrs Cantrip. I'd advise you to go home. They can put through any calls that come in.'

It might take days, it might take weeks, but eventually Twohey would be found. And then, Wexford thought as he drove past the King's School, he would talk. He would sit in Wexford's office, staring at the expanse of pale blue sky through the picture window as hundreds of unscrupulous villains had sat and stared before him, but, unlike most of them, he would have no reason to hold his tongue. A long term of imprisonment awaited him whether he spoke or kept silent. Probably he would be glad to talk to revenge himself on the dead woman and all her family, for no more money would come his way from that source.

And what would he say? That Villiers' love for his brother-in-law was of a kind that their narrow society couldn't condone? That Elizabeth had had a series of lovers young enough to be her own children? Or that, long ago, Villiers and Elizabeth had been concerned together in a criminal conspiracy?

Suddenly Wexford remembered the bombed house in which their parents had died. They were only children then, but children had been known to commit murder . . . Two people buried under rubble but still alive, parents who were perhaps a stumbling block in the way of their children's ambition. Certainly Villiers had benefited greatly from their deaths. His sister hadn't. Did the clue lie there?

Twohey would know. It was terribly frustrating to Wexford to think that perhaps Twohey was the only person now alive who did know and that he was hidden away comfortably with his secret. And it might be days, it might be weeks. . . .

On to Myfleet. The church bells of Clusterwell were ringing for Evensong and, as soon as their chimes died away behind him, he heard those of Myfleet ahead, eight bells ringing great brazen changes through the evening air.

There was a note pinned to Mrs Cantrip's front door: *Gone to church. Back 7.30.* An invitation to burglars, Wexford thought, only he couldn't remember any burglary taking place in Myfleet for ten years. Its trees shrouded crimes of greater moment. He turned away, and the ginger cat, locked out among the flowers, rubbed itself against his legs.

Breathing in the scent of the pines that all day had been bathed in sunshine. Wexford entered the forest. The path he took was the path Elizabeth Nightingale had taken that night, and he followed it until he came to the clearing where Burden believed she had met Twohey and he believed—what?

Perhaps Burden was right again, after all. Those parcels might never have been posted but delivered by hand. She would hardly have carried such large sums of money loose in her handbag. Anyway, she hadn't had a handbag, only a coat and a torch . . . He stared at the lichened log where she had sat. The scrape marks of four shoes were still apparent on the dry sandy ground and in the whorls of pine needles four shifting feet had made.

If her companion was Twohey—observed perhaps by Sean who misunderstood the purpose of their meeting—how had Twohey come? Over the black wooded hill from Pomfret? Or by the path that skirted the Myfleet cottage gardens and came out eventually—where? Wexford decided to explore it.

The church bells had stopped and the place was utterly silent. He walked between the straight narrow pine trunks, looking up sometimes at the patches of pale silvery sky, and sometimes from side to side of him into the forest itself which was so dark and, up to head height, so sterile, that no birds sang there and the only visible life was that of the midges which danced in swarms.

It was on account of the midges that he was glad when the trees to the left of him petered out and he found himself walking against the cottage fences. Presently, ahead of him, he heard a whisper of music. It was a sentimental treacly melody that he soon defined as belonging to the pop or dance-music order, and it reminded Wexford of those soft and faintly erotic tunes which had floated down to him from Katje Doorn's transistor. Just as he was thinking how pleasant and undemanding it sounded on this peaceful summer evening, it ceased and was succeeded by an appalling cacophony, the furious result of several saxophones, organs, drums and electric guitars all being played at once.

Wexford put his head over the fence and stared into the square plot of land, part wilderness and part rubbish dump, which was the Lovells' back garden. From the open kitchen window some fifty feet of electric lead stretched to the shed from which the noise emanated. Wexford backed a little, covering his assaulted ears.

Then he took his hands down.

Inside the shed someone was speaking. The tone and timbre of the voice were unmistakable, its accent deliberately cultivated. Mid-Atlantic, Wexford decided.

With mounting curiosity, he listened.

Addressing his unseen, indeed non-existent, audience as 'guys and dolls', Sean Lovell, with smooth professional patter, made a short dismissive comment on the last piece of music and then, more enthusiastically, announced his next record. This time it was the effusion of a big band and it was even more discordant than the composition which had made Wexford cover his ears.

It stopped. Sean spoke again and, as he took in the full

implication of his words, a shaft of intense pity pierced Wexford. Perhaps, he thought, there are few things so sad as eavesdropping on a man alone with his daydreams, a man indulging his solitary, private and ridiculous vice.

'And now,' said the disembodied voice, 'what you've all been waiting for. You've come a long way tonight and I can promise you you're not going to be disappointed. Here he is, boys and girls. Let's have a big hand for your own Sean Lovell!'

Unaccompanied, he began to sing. Wexford walked away, very delicately and softly for such a big man, his feet scarcely causing a crackle on the needled forest floor.

He knew now what Sean had been doing that night, what he did every night and would perhaps do for years until some girl caught him and showed him how daydreams die and that life is digging a rich man's garden.

15

WEXFORD was so tired that he fell asleep as soon as his head was on the pillow. Like most people approaching that phase of life which succeeds middle age but is not yet old age, he was finding it more and more difficult to get a good night's sleep. Years ago, when he was still young, he had acquired the sensible habit of emptying his mind at night of all the speculations and worries which troubled him during the day, and of turning his thoughts to future domestic plans or back to pleasant memories. But his subconscious was outside his control and it often asserted itself in dreams of those daytime anxieties.

So it was that night. In his dream he was down by the Kingsbrook, the scene of many of his favourite walks, when he saw a boy fishing upstream. The boy was fair and thin with a strong-boned Anglo-Saxon face. Wexford went nearer to him, keeping in the shadow of the trees, for some inexplicable dream reason not wishing to be observed. It was pleasant and warm down by the river, a summer evening that, he felt, had succeeded a long hot day.

Presently he heard someone calling and he saw a girl come running over the brow of the hill. Her light, almost yellow, hair and the cast of her face told him she was the boy's sister, older than he, perhaps fourteen or fifteen. She had come to fetch him away, and he heard them break into bitter argument because the boy wanted to remain and go on fishing.

He knew he had to follow them across the meadows. They ran ahead of him, the girl's hair flying. Above him a plane zoomed over, and he saw the bombs dropping like heavy black feathers.

Something of the house still remained standing, bare windowless walls enclosing a smoking mass from which came the cries of those buried alive. The children were neither shocked nor frightened, for this was a nightmare where natural emotions are suspended. He watched, a detached observer, as the girl groped her way into the black inferno, the boy at her heels. Now he could see a long pale arm protrude from the rubble and hear a voice calling for help, for mercy. The children began shovelling with their bare hands and he came closer to help them. Then he saw that they were not uncovering the screaming faces but burying them deeper, laughing like demons as they worked furiously to finish what the bomb had begun, and he jerked awake as he shouted to them to stop.

Conscious now, he found himself sitting up, his shouts coming as half-choked snores. His wife, lying beside him, hadn't stirred. He rubbed his eyes and looked at the luminous hands of his watch. It was five past two.

If he awoke at that hour he knew he would never get to sleep again and his usual habit was to go downstairs, sit in an armchair and find something to read. The dream stayed with him, vivid and haunting, as he put on his dressing gown and made for the stairs. In the morning he would set in motion the research necessary to discover exactly what had happened that day the Villiers' home was destroyed. Now for something to read . . .

As a young man, when he had had more spare time and less responsibility, he had been a great reader, and literary criticism and writers' biographies had been among his favourite reading matter. Mrs Wexford couldn't understand this and he remembered how she had asked him why he wanted to read what someone else said about a book. Why not just read the book itself? And he hadn't quite known how to answer her, how in this field he couldn't trust his own judgment because he was only a policeman and he hadn't a university degree. Nor could he have told her that he needed instruction and knowledge because the purpose of education is to turn the soul's eye towards the light.

Thinking of this and of the pleasure he had had from such works, he turned his physical eye to *Wordsworth in Love* which he had left lying on the coffee table. After only four hours' sleep he was no longer tired and far more alert than when he had formerly tried to apply himself to this book. He might as well have another go at it. Pity it was about Wordsworth, though. Rather a dull poet, he thought. All that communing with nature and walking about in the Lake District. A bit tedious really. Now if only it had been about Lord Byron, say, that would have been a different matter, something to get his teeth into. There was an interesting character for you, a romantic larger-than-life man with his sizzling love affairs, his disastrous marriage, the scandal over Augusta Leigh. Still, it wasn't; it was about Wordsworth. Well, he would read it and maybe, even if it bored him, he would get some idea of the nature of the fascination the Lake poet had for Villiers, the obsession almost that had made him write God knew how many books about him.

He began to read and this time he found it easy and pleasant to follow. After a while he began to wish he had read more of Wordsworth's poetry. He had no idea the man had been in love with a French girl, had been involved in the Revolution and had narrowly missed losing his head. It was good, bracing stuff and Villiers wrote well.

At six he made himself a large pot of tea. He read on, utterly absorbed, and by now considerably excited. The room began to fill with light, and slowly, with the same gradual dawning, Wexford's mind was illuminated. He finished the last chapter and closed the book.

Sighing, he addressed himself coldly, 'You ignorant old fool!' Then he rubbed his stiff hands and said aloud, 'If only it had been Byron! My God, if only it had. I would have known the answer long ago.'

'The first Monday morning of term,' said John Burden, finishing his third slice of toast and marmalade, 'is worse than the first *day* of term.' And he added gloomily: 'Things really start getting serious.' He prodded his sister with a sticky finger. 'Isn't it time you started being sick?'

'I'm not going to be sick, you beast.'

'Why ever not? Today's worse than the first day, much, much worse. I bet you'll be ever so sick when you start at the High School. *If* you get there. You'll be too sick to do the exams.'

'I shan't!'

'Oh, yes, you will.'

'Be quiet, the pair of you,' said Burden. 'Sometimes I think there's more peace and quiet down at the nick.' He left the breakfast table and prepared to go there. 'You must be the most unnatural brother and sister in Sussex,' he said.

John looked pleased at being placed in this unique category. 'Can I have a lift, Dad? Old Roman Villa's taking us for Prayers and there'll be hell to pay if I'm late.'

'Don't say "hell to pay",' said Burden absently. 'Come on, then. I've got a busy day ahead of me.'

A day of hunting for a needle in a haystack, of running a predator to earth. He marched into the police station and met Sergeant Martin in the foyer.

'Anything turned up on Twohey yet?'

'No, sir, not as far as I know, but Mr Wexford's on to something. He said he wanted to see you as soon as you came in.'

Burden went up in the lift.

The chief inspector was sitting at his desk, impatiently drumming his fingers on the blotter. There were pouches under his eyes and he looked, Burden thought, very much the worse for wear. And yet, about his whole demeanour, there was an air of triumph, of momentous discovery that until this moment he had kept suppressed.

'You're late,' he snapped. 'I've had to go over and swear out the warrant myself.'

'What warrant? You mean you've found Twohey?'

'Twohey be damned,' said Wexford, jumping up and taking his raincoat from the stand. 'Hasn't it yet penetrated your dapper little skull that this is a *murder* hunt? We are going to Clusterwell to make an arrest.'

Obediently, Burden followed him from the room. Wexford didn't care for the lift and, since he had been trapped in it for two hours one afternoon, had tended to avoid it. But now he jumped in and pressed the button apparently without a qualm.

'Villiers' place?' Burden asked and, when Wexford nodded, 'Well, you won't find him there. He's taking school Prayers this morning.'

'How bloody unsuitable.' Wexford gave an explosive snort. The lift sank gently and the door slid open. 'We'll take one of the W.P.C.s with us, Mike.'

'Shall we indeed? When are you going to tell me who we're arresting and why?'

'In the car,' said Wexford. 'On the way.'

'And how you suddenly happened to see the light?'

Wexford smiled a smile full of triumph and renewed confidence. 'I couldn't sleep,' he said as they waited for the policewoman to join them. 'I couldn't sleep, so I read a book. I'm an ignorant old policeman, Mike. I don't read enough. I should have read this one when its author first gave it to me.'

'I didn't know it was a detective story, sir,' said Burden innocently.

'Don't be so bloody silly,' Wexford snapped. 'I don't mean the book outlines the murder plan. Anyway, there was no plan.'

'Of course not. It was unpremeditated.'

'Yes, you were right there and right about a lot of things,' Wexford said, adding in a sudden burst of confidence: 'I don't mind telling you, I began to think you were right in everything. I thought I was getting old, past it.'

'Oh, come, sir,' said Burden heartily. 'That's nonsense.'

'Yes, it is,' the chief inspector snapped. 'I've still got my eyesight, I've still got some intuition. Well, don't stand hanging about there all day. We've got to make an arrest.'

Someone else must have stood on the dais and commanded the boys to lift up their hearts and voices, for Denys Villiers was at home.

'I took the day off,' he said to Wexford. 'I'm not well.'

'You look ill, Mr Villiers,' said Wexford gravely and, meeting the man's eyes, 'You always look ill.'

'Do I? Yes, perhaps I do.'

'You don't seem curious about the purpose of our call.'

Villiers threw up his head. 'I'm not. I know why you've come.'

'I should like to see your wife.'

'I know that too. Do you imagine I think you've brought a policewoman for the sake of a little feminine company? You underrate your opponent, Mr Wexford.'

'You have always underrated yours.'

Villiers gave a slight painful smile. 'Yes, we have been a mutual denigration society.' He went to the bedroom door. 'Georgina!'

She came out, shoulders hunched, head bent. Wexford had only once before seen anyone come through a doorway like that, and then it had been a man, a father who for two days had kept his children at gunpoint in a room with him. At last he had been persuaded to drop his gun and come out, walk across the threshold to the waiting police and crumple into his wife's arms.

Georgina crumpled into her husband's.

He held her in a close embrace and he stroked her hair. Wexford heard her murmuring to him, begging him not to leave her. She wore no jewellery but her wedding and engagement rings.

It was so painful to watch that he couldn't bring himself to speak the words of the charge. He stood awkwardly, clearing his throat, giving a little cough like the sound he had made when she had locked herself in the bathroom. Suddenly she lifted her head and looked at them over her husband's shoulder. Tears were pouring down her freckled cheeks.

'Yes, I killed Elizabeth,' she said hoarsely. 'The torch was on the ground. I picked it up and killed her. I'm glad I did it.' Denys Villiers, still holding her, shivered violently. 'If I had known before, I would have killed her sooner. I killed her as soon as I knew.'

Very quietly Wexford spoke the words of the charge.

'I don't care what you take down in writing,' she said. 'I did it because I wanted to keep my husband. He's mine, he belongs to me. I never had anyone else to belong to me. She had everything but I only had him.'

Villiers listened with a still set face. 'May I go with her?' Wexford had never expected to hear him speak so humbly.

'Of course you may,' he said.

The policewoman took Georgina to the waiting car, an arm round her shoulders. The arm was only for support and to prevent her from stumbling, but it looked as if it had been placed there from kindness and a kind of sisterly regard. Burden followed them, walking with the slow stiff pace of a mourner at a funeral.

Villiers looked at Wexford and the chief inspector returned his gaze. 'She can't tell you very much,' said Villiers. 'I'm the only person living who knows it all.'

'Yes, Mr Villiers, we shall need to take a statement from you.'

'I've written something already. Other people talk or else shut it all up inside themselves, but writers write. I wrote this in the night. I haven't been able to sleep. I haven't slept at all.'

And the envelope was waiting on the hall table, propped against a vase. Taking it, Wexford saw that it was addressed to him and that there was a stamp on it.

'If you hadn't come this morning I should have posted it. I couldn't have borne the waiting any longer. Now you have it I think perhaps I shall sleep.'

'Shall we go, then?' said Wexford.

Burden drove with Villiers beside him. No one spoke. As they entered Kingsmarkham, Wexford slit open the envelope and glanced briefly at the first typewritten sheet

Then the car swung on to the police station forecourt.

He got out and opened the nearside front door. But Villiers didn't move. Touching his shoulder to tell him they had arrived, Wexford saw with a sudden shaft of compassion, the first he had ever felt for the man, that Villiers was fast asleep.

For the attention of Chief Inspector Wexford

I cannot suppose that I am among your favourite authors, so I will keep this statement as brief as I can. I am writing it at night while my wife sleeps. Yes, she can sleep, the sleep of the innocent, just avenger.

When you quoted Byron to me I was sure that you knew why if you did not know how. But I have asked myself since then, did you know? Did you even know what you were saying? I stared at you. I waited for you to arrest my wife, and my face must have told you what I was afraid of: that you, to frighten me and to extract a confession from me, had quoted to me the words of a man all the world knows to have been his sister's lover.

I think I betrayed myself then. I certainly did so when I gave you my book to read. But then I thought you were too ignorant, too dull and plodding, to equate a short passage in my book with my own life. Now, as the dawn comes up and in its light I look at things coldly and dispassionately, as I remind myself of my provocative rudeness to you and your civilised forbearance, as I remember your percipience, I know that I was wrong. You will read and you will realise, 'Thou best philosopher, thou eye among the blind!'

Wordsworth wrote that, Mr Wexford. Wordsworth, as you now know, also loved his own sister, but being a disciple of duty (stern daughter of the voice of God), he left her. You will no longer need to ask what attracted me to Wordsworth, in what particular our affinity lay. For, although Dorothy appears in my book as the merest interlude between Annette and Mary, you will have noted the parallel; you will have realised what, when I was a young man, seeking a subject to which I might devote my life, drew me to this poet. That among other things, of course. I consider Wordsworth second only to Milton and can say with Coleridge, 'Wordsworth is a very great man, the only man to whom at all times and in all modes of excellence I feel myself inferior.'

I might, of course, have chosen Lord Byron. The obviousness of the choice repelled me. Besides, I did not want to waste my muse on one whom I consider superficial and grandiloquent, a swashbuckling pop star, simply because he had committed incest (very probably) with Augusta Leigh. But Byron, *because* he is better known now for his incest than his verse, affects me strangely, the very mention of his name, the quotation of his lines, sets my nerves on edge. You could say that I am allergic to him.

But I am forgetting my promise to be brief.

When we were children I did not love my sister. We were always quarrelling and our separation caused us no distress. We were glad to get shot of each other. I did not see her again until I was in my last year at Oxford.

Our meeting was at the twenty-first birthday party of a university acquaintance of mine. This man's father introduced me to his secretary, a girl called Elizabeth Langham. We went out together and soon we became lovers.

I told you I was a good liar but I am not lying now when I say that I had no idea who she really was or that I had ever seen her before the night of this party. Nine years had passed and we had altered. I asked her to marry me and then she had to tell me. For two months I had been my own sister's lover.

For years she had followed my fortunes, from envy and a sense of the unfairness of the arrangement that had been made for us. Having run away to London with a man called Langham who had paid for her to take a secretarial course, she took a job with my friend's father, knowing that his son and I were at Oxford together. She went to the party, curious to see me; she came out with me with some unformed plan of revenge in her mind. But then the situation passed out of her control. In spite of what she knew, she had fallen in love with me. Did it trouble her? I don't think so. Long before this she had passed far beyond the confines of accepted morality, so that she saw this step only as something especially daring and defiant of society.

We parted, she to America with her employer, I to Oxford. I will not dwell on my feelings at this time. You are a sensitive man and perhaps you can imagine them for yourself.

I married as soon as I had my degree; not for love—I have never in my life been in love with anyone but Elizabeth—but for safety, for normality. The allowance my uncle had made me ceased when I was twenty-one, so, knowing that I could never make a living from writing poetry or from writing about it, I applied for a teaching job at the King's School.

Was I taking a risk in returning to Kingsmarkham? Elizabeth had told me she hated the place. I thought I had found the one town in the world my sister would be sure to avoid.

It was that egregious busyboy, Lionel Marriott, who

told me Elizabeth was here. I dreaded meeting her; I longed to see her. We met. She introduced me to her husband, the son of a millionaire who had been on holiday in America while she was working there. He had bought the Manor as a surprise for her, believing she would like to live near her childhood home.

We sat at table together with her husband and my wife. We made small talk. As soon as our chance came we saw each other alone, and that, Mr Wexford, was the second beginning.

Our love would have been impossible without the innocent acquiescence of Quentin Nightingale. If he had disliked me it would have been difficult for Elizabeth and me to have met and, since I could not have borne to live near her but separated from her, I should have been forced to change my job and move away. I wish with all my heart now that this had happened.

Women are tougher than we are, less scrupulous, less a prey to guilt. I suppose Elizabeth had been in love with Quentin when she married him and had meant to be an honest faithful wife. Immediately I re-entered her life she put all this behind her and began to use him as a tool. Her aim was to have me as her lover and at the same time to keep her position, her money and her reputation. She wanted the best of both worlds and she got them Still, to shift the blame like this is useless. I was as guilty as she. The difference between us was that I had a con science and she had none.

She worked on Quentin in devious and subtle ways. She told him, pretending that June was her source, that I wa a difficult man with a disturbed personality. It would b a kindness on his part to befriend me. Characteristically he reacted by offering me a room in the Old House for my exclusive use.

It was to seem as if all my invitations to the Manor came from Quentin, for Elizabeth and I must appear to dislike each other. Why? She said that if we showed even normal fraternal affection in public we should soon be betrayed into showing a deeper love than is permitted to brother and sister. I do not believe this was her true reason. Rather, I think, she loved intrigue for its own sake and our public indifference lent for her a spice to our private love.

And if I say that I loved Quentin too will you call this the vilest hypocrisy? Or has your experience taught you that it is often those whom we have betrayed and deceived and dishonoured that we love the best? For, in preventing them from discovering our betrayal, we learn how to protect them from other harm as well as this one, and the kind words we use initially to blind them become habitual and ultimately sincere. Yes, Mr Wexford, I loved Quentin, and Elizabeth, who discouraged all my friendships lest I should be driven to confide in a friend, allowed me this one, never understanding that of all mankind he was the man I longed to confess to, his the only forgiveness I should have valued.

I shall now come to Twohey.

He had been watching Elizabeth visit me at the Old House, and one day he saw me walk down the stairs with her and embrace her in the apple room. It was not a brother's embrace and Twohey, from outside the window, took a photograph. I paid him blackmail. When he had bled me white Elizabeth began selling her jewellery and having copies made.

You have not found Twohey yet, have you? Let me help you. Apart from saving Georgina as much suffering as I can, I have only one wish left and that is to see Twohey as wretched as he made Elizabeth and me. You will find his address on the dressmaker's bills in the writing desk in her bedroom. Tanya Tye is the name (more probably the alias) of the woman with whom he lives in a luxury flat over the shop in Bruton Street. It was all quite simple and very clever. Whenever Twohey wanted money he would send Elizabeth a bill from Tanya Tye and the money she was to pay was the sum on the bill *plus* one nought added to the figure. For example: if the bill was for a hundred and fifty pounds, Elizabeth was to send him fifteen hundred. She sent the money in brown paper parcels. The last one was posted by Katje the day before Elizabeth died. To show her he had received the money he sent her receipted bills.

Good hunting, Mr Wexford.

I suppose Marriott has enlightened you as to all the details of my surface life. You will know that the Nightingales and I always took our holidays together and that two years ago, because of Quentin's illness, Elizabeth and I went away alone. Marriott said we looked ill and careworn when we came home from Dubrovnik, but it never occurred to him that we were sick at heart, not because we had quarrelled but because we had been happy.

I wanted her to leave Quentin and come away with me. She refused. Had we set up house together years ago no one would have suspected that we were brother and sister. Now everyone knew it and the scandal would be monumental. That is what she said. But I knew her so well, *soror mea sponsor*. I knew that her money and her position meant as much to her as I did. She was used to her two worlds, her eggs in two baskets, and, leaving out her terror of Twohey, I think she was mostly happy.

I had come to the end. I was thirty-six and all my life

I had worked hard but I had nothing. The fruits of all my labours had gone to keep a Mayfair modiste's lover in luxury; I had no wife, no children, no friends and I lived in three rooms. True, I had Elizabeth, but for how long? The time would come when she, tranquillised by middle age, would sacrifice me to her other, safer world.

I decided to make a complete break, so I refused all Quentin's invitations to the Manor, his almost irresistible pleas. I thought I should be able to work. Instead I lay evening after evening on my bed, thinking, doing nothing, sometimes contemplating suicide. It was a dark night of the soul, comparable to the breakdown Wordsworth had when he had to leave France and leave Annette behind.

I no longer wanted Elizabeth. If I missed either of them it was Quentin that I missed. I went to the Manor at last and told them I would not go to Rome with them. I looked at Elizabeth and felt—nothing. It was incomprehensible to me that I had wasted the best of my life in loving her.

I went to Spain. Not the romantic, magic Spain of Madrid and the high sierras, but the sweltering Blackpool which is what we have made of the Costa Brava, and I went as escort to the school party. I suppose I told myself that to feel rage and exasperation and excruciating boredom would be better than to feel nothing at all.

Georgina was staying at the same hotel. I am no longer an attractive man, Mr Wexford, and I look much older than I am. I have no conversation, for I have talked my whole soul out to my sister. Long long ago I lost the technique of talking beguilingly to young women. I am better suited to a Trappist's cell than to caper nimbly in a lady's chamber. But Georgina fell in love with me, poor thing. It was quite a joke in that horrible hotel, Georgina's love.

I had had everything and, rich in gifts, had squandered

them all. She had never had anything. The youngest child of a large poor family, she told me that she had never possessed anything she could feel to be exclusively her own. No man had ever wanted her or even taken her out more than a couple of times. She was plain and shy and dull.

A poor ill-favoured thing, but mine own . . .

We were married. I brought Georgina to the Manor and to the disappointment in Quentin's eyes. Elizabeth suffered no disappointment. She was triumphant in her white velvet and her fake jewels. I looked at her, I looked at poor Georgina and I asked myself, as once again I fell in love with my sister, what have I done?

The third beginning and the last. . . .

I wanted to settle down. I wanted those children. If not six, I wanted some. But I did not listen to the stern daughter of God's voice, nor even to the shriller querulous voice of my wife, clamouring for me to be all in all to her, a compensation for long loneliness, a real husband who would cherish her. I listened to my sister.

So we come to the day of Elizabeth's death.

No, of course you did not believe me when I said I went down to the school library in the evenings to do research for my work. Only someone as innocent and as uninterested in literature as Georgina would believe that. My own works on Wordsworth are the only ones in the school library, apart from the Selincourt and Darbyshire collection edition and those volumes I have in my own house. I went to meet Elizabeth in the forest.

We had spent the afternoon of that day together, but that was not enough for us. The school holidays would soon be over and then . . . ? Weekly bridge parties; Literary discussions with Quentin, and Elizabeth a silent third? We were sick for each other. We arranged to meet in the forest at eleven.

I have said that Georgina accepted my excuses, but if she had, Elizabeth would be alive today. Georgina had begun to doubt me and to a woman as possessive as she, doubt calls for action.

We went to the Manor and played bridge. Just before we left Elizabeth gave Georgina a silk scarf. She used to give Georgina a lot of her cast-off clothing. I suppose it amused her to see my wife in handed-on finery, knowing that Georgina would look less well in it than she and that I would notice and make the obvious unjust comparison.

I drove Georgina home and went out again to meet Elizabeth. She came to the clearing in the wood just before eleven. We sat on a log, we smoked, we talked. Elizabeth had brought with her that torch from the garden room, for the moon had gone in and it was dark.

At about twenty past she said that we should go. Georgina's faint display of temper after our bridge game had made her nervous and she said to spend too long in the forest would be to tempt Providence.

It was my usual practice, after these meetings of ours, to wait by my car and watch her cross the road and gain the safety of the Manor grounds, so we walked to the car together with our arms round each other. As we went we saw the headlights of another car moving on the road, as if searching the fringe of the forest with its beams. It passed on and we forgot it.

When we came to my car Elizabeth said that she had forgotten her torch and must go back for it, in case someone should find it and know she had been there. I wanted to go with her, but she said she would be safe alone. What, after all, could happen to her? What indeed?

I took her in my arms and kissed her, just as I had

kissed her on the day Twohey was outside the window. Then I drove home. Georgina was not there when I got back; nor was her car. She came in at midnight, shivering in a thin shirt—for she had burnt her sweater on Palmer's bonfire—and in her hand she held a bloodstained torch wrapped up in newspaper.

She had followed me, Mr Wexford, and seen me kiss Elizabeth, so she waited by the log for Elizabeth to come back for the torch. What happened then I only know from what Georgina told me. She was so shocked by what she had seen, so horrified, that the balance of her mind, as coroners put it, was disturbed. She tried to express this to Elizabeth, but she was incoherent, she was hysterical, and Elizabeth laughed at her. What did she, Georgina, think she could do about it? she asked her. We would not, in the nature of things, be lovers for ever. Georgina must wait and one day I would return to her. Surely she would not risk the scandal that would arise if she made scenes or told anyone?

Elizabeth bent over to find the torch which she thought had fallen behind the log. It had not. Georgina was holding it and, while Elizabeth had her back to her, she raised it and struck my sister. Again and again until Elizabeth was dead.

Georgina was wearing the scarf herself. She pulled it off and wiped her own hands with it. Then she crossed the road, stuffed the scarf into a hollow tree and burnt her sweater on Palmer's bonfire.

Is that not nearly all? When Georgina came home and told me what she had done, I confessed the whole story to her. I told her about the blackmail and about the jewels.

I know what you are asking me. Why didn't I, as my sister's lover and dearest friend, immediately give my wife up to you? And you have provided your own

190

answer, that I was afraid of the relationship becoming known. But it was not entirely that. I was almost stunned with horror, with grief, and yet even then I wanted to salvage my life. With Elizabeth gone, I might yet settle down, be peaceful, be happy, tell no more lies.

Man is a strange creature, Mr Wexford. He has lifted himself so far above his fellow animals that Darwin's Theory seems fantastic to him, a monstrous libel. And yet he still shares with them his strongest instinct, self-preservation. The whole world may lie in ruins about him, but still he looks for a corner to run into and clings to his hope that it can never, no matter what bombardment he has suffered, be too late.

At that moment I loathed Georgina. I could have beaten her to death. But I told myself that what had happened was my fault. I had done it. I did it when I went to that party so many years ago. So, instead of doing violence to her, I took her in my arms and smelt Elizabeth's blood in her hair and under her fingernails.

I washed the torch myself and threw away the wet batteries. I ran a bath for Georgina and told her to wash her hair. The skirt she had been wearing and her shirt I burned on the kitchen boiler.

I could not see why you should suspect Georgina, for she had no apparent motive, and that is why I grew hysterical when you brought us the news of the will. To arrest my wife and convict her for the wrong motive! That would have been the ultimate irony.

She was very nervous, very bad at countering your attacks. When we were alone she told me she would like to confess, for you or any right-thinking person would understand. I prevented her. I thought we still had a chance. Then you quoted Lara to me and I began to make notes in preparation for this statement.

It is all over now.

You will, I am sure, be gentle with Georgina, and I know that during her trial every newspaper reader in this country will be for her heart and soul, as well as those more significant arbiters, the judge and jury. She will go to prison for two or three years and then one day she will marry again, have the children she needs and the normal quiet life she wants. June re-married long ago. Soon Quentin will have his little Dutch girl as chatelaine of Myfleet and, if she is unfaithful to him, it will be a natural run-of-the-mill infidelity that my kind brother will bear with a perhaps not too painful fortitude. As for Elizabeth, she died at the height of her love and her triumph and just in time to avoid the bitterness of growing old.

Indeed, one might say with Wilde that the good ended happily and the bad unhappily, for that is the meaning of fiction. Perhaps it should also be the meaning of fact. In other words, I have my deserts. I have no idea what I shall do, but I think it unlikely that after the trial any authority will wish to employ me on its teaching staff.

I care very little about that. I think I can bear scandal without too much distress, and if people shun me I can do without people. The one person I cannot do without I shall never see again, and this thing which is unbearable I must bear. I shall never again kiss her in the dark forest or among the shadows of the Old House or see her dressed in white velvet or hear her name spoken with admiration. She is dead and her death is for me the ultimate irreparable mutilation.

Your inspector asked me what I wanted and nothing has happened to make me change my answer. I want to die.